'Engrossing story with a real insight into the world of pre-teen girls.'

Publishing News

'Rising star Judi Curtin's *Alice* books celebrate friendship, humour and loyalty.'

Sunday Independent

JUDI CURTIN grew up in Cork and now lives in Limerick where she is married with three children. Judi is the best-selling author of the 'Alice & Megan' series and of *Eva's Journey* and *Eva's Holiday*; with Roisin Meaney, she is also the author of *See If I Care*, and she has written three novels, *Sorry, Walter*, *From Claire to Here* and *Almost Perfect*. Her books have sold into Serbian, Portuguese, German, Russian and Lithuanian, and into Australia and New Zealand.

The 'Alice & Megan' series

Alice Next Door

Alice Again

Don't Ask Alice

Alice in the Middle

Bonjour Alice

Alice & Megan Forever

Alice to the Rescue

Alice & Megan's Cookbook

Other books

Eva's Journey

Eva's Holiday

See If I Care (with Roisin Meaney)

Alice Next Door

Judi Curtin

Illustrations: Woody Fox

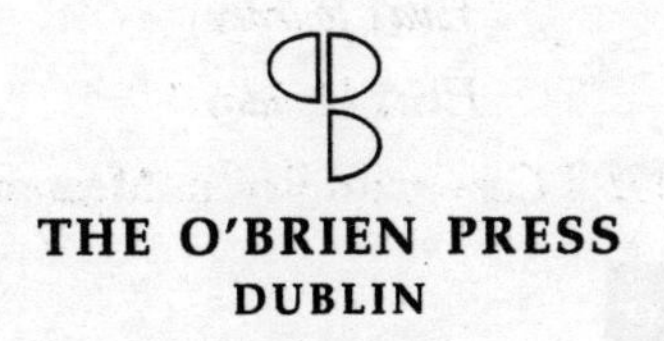

THE O'BRIEN PRESS
DUBLIN

First published 2005 by The O'Brien Press Ltd,
12 Terenure Road East, Rathgar, Dublin 6, Ireland.
Tel: +353 1 4923333; Fax: +353 1 4922777
E-mail: books@obrien.ie
Website: www.obrien.ie
Reprinted 2005, 2006, 2008, 2010, 2011.

ISBN: 978-0-86278-898-8

British Library Cataloguing-in-Publication Data
A catalogue record for this title is available from The British Library

6 7 8 9
11 12 13 14

Illustrations: Woody Fox
Layout and design: The O'Brien Press Ltd
Printing: Cox & Wyman Ltd
The paper used in this book is produced using pulp from managed forests

The O'Brien Press receives assistance from

DEDICATION

For Mum and Dad.

ACKNOWLEDGEMENTS

Big thanks, as usual, to Dan, Annie, Ellen and Brian. Thanks to David, Sarah, Eoin and Alison for being great nieces and nephews. To everyone at The O'Brien Press, thanks for all your hard work.

Extra-special thanks to the children from Limerick School Project, and Milford NS, who listened to this story, and laughed in all the right places.

Chapter one

Sheila Sheehan says that I'm the most beautiful girl in the world. She says my eyes are the prettiest shade of blue she's ever seen. Sometimes she combs my hair for me and she says it's the silkiest hair she's ever touched in all her life.

She has to say all that stuff though. She's my mum. It's her job.

My mum has a lot to say on every subject. Sometimes I tell her to lighten up, but she only gives me her exasperated look, and continues anyway.

Mum says that my best friend Alice's mum is an evil, selfish cow.

But she only says that when she thinks I'm not listening.

It doesn't matter anyway. Alice and her mum have gone to live in Dublin. Her dad still lives next door to us, but that's not much good to me, is it? He won't want to take basketball shots with me, or to play Monopoly, or to lie on the floor of my room listening to music, and laughing at nothing.

At first, when Alice told me she was leaving, I hoped that she'd be down to see her dad at weekends. We could still be friends. That's the way it works in books anyway. Or in films – as long as they're rated PG. Real life wasn't turning out like that though. Alice's mum pulled what my mum calls her master-stroke. She enrolled Alice and her brother, Jamie, in piano classes on Saturday afternoons. That means that they can't come to Limerick at all, except at holiday time, and for long weekends. If Alice's dad wants to see her any other time, he'll have to go all the way to Dublin. It's September now, and the next long weekend isn't for weeks and weeks and weeks.

Mum says not to get my hopes up too much because Veronica, (that's Alice's mum) will probably find some reason not to send the kids to see their dad. But I have to hope. What else can I do?

And I have to face into school tomorrow. It'll be the first time ever without Alice in my class. We started together in junior infants, and have been together ever since. We were together when Alice spilt milk on her trousers and had to change into the horrible brown scratchy ones the teacher kept in the cupboard under the nature table. And everyone else thought she'd wet her knickers.

Alice never laughed at me when my mum gave me carrot sticks and broccoli for school lunch. With a bottle of water to wash it all down.

Alice was the only one who didn't tease me when I had to go to school in darned tights because Mum said it was a waste to throw them out just because of one small hole. (I said I'd skip on the organic porridge for a week and spend the savings on new tights, but Mum didn't think that was funny.)

I never laughed at Alice when her mum forgot to pack any lunch at all for her, and the teacher had to ask all the kids to share and everyone offered the worst, soggy, squashed thing in their lunchboxes. Once she had to take an egg sandwich from Tom, who hadn't washed his hands in about five hundred years. Luckily I was able to distract him while she threw it into the bin. That's what friends are for, isn't it?

* * *

Alice and her mum left yesterday. It had been planned for weeks though. Alice's mum said she was leaving Alice's dad because they just couldn't get on. 'Irreconcilable differences', was what she said.

My mum said that if Alice's dad got the big promotion and the new silver BMW she'd been hoping for, they'd have got on just fine. She said

Alice's mum was a social climber of the highest order. She'd never be happy living in a three-bedroomed semi, and driving around in a four-year-old car.

Of course, Mum didn't think I was listening when she said all of this on the phone to my aunt Linda. She should be more careful.

Anyway, it was awful when Alice left. If it was a film, I suppose I'd have cried and hugged her and we would have promised to be friends forever. I couldn't though. Alice and I weren't huggy kind of girls. I just felt very sad.

'Bye, Al,' I said.

'Bye, Meg,' she said.

Usually there wasn't enough time to say all the things I wanted to say to Alice. Right then though, I couldn't think of anything else to say.

She looked sad too. 'Don't forget to send me lots of e-mails.'

'Oh yeah. I will. I mean I won't forget. I promise. I'll send lots of e-mails. Every day.'

Alice smiled a funny, stiff kind of smile.

'And don't forget to say "hi" to Melissa for me.'

I groaned. Melissa is the meanest girl in the world. Alice and I have both hated her since forever. Now I'd have to hate her all on my own. And that's no fun.

Alice's mum put her fancy light brown designer handbag on the front seat of the car and then she sat into the driver's seat. She turned the driving mirror towards herself and fixed her hair. Then she put on some lipstick. Imagine, putting on lipstick for a drive to Dublin. Did she think it would show up on the speed cameras?

'Come on, Alice. If we don't go soon we'll be stuck in traffic all afternoon. It'll be teatime before we get through Castletroy.'

It was Saturday, so that was a stupid thing to say. Even I knew there were never traffic jams on Saturdays. Alice didn't argue though. She just got into the car, and helped Jamie with his seat belt. Then her mum started the engine, and they drove off.

I waved until they were out of sight. That didn't take long. They live right at the top of the road and they were gone in about three and a half seconds.

Mum hugged me as we went inside, and offered to make me a fruit smoothie. As if that would help. Even a huge Coke wouldn't have made me feel better, and there was fat chance of getting one of those.

Later Mum took me shopping. We went to O'Mahony's bookshop and she bought me two new books. Then she bought me a new T-shirt, a spotty scrunchie and a comic. When she bought the comic I knew she must be feeling really sorry for me. Last time she bought me a comic was when my goldfish died. (The fish had gone a really revolting black colour, and had big warty lumps all down its back. I was glad it was dead. But luckily Mum didn't know that. And the comic more than made up for the loss of the fish.) This was different though. A year's supply of comics wouldn't have helped. No point in reading a comic on my own. Reading comics was only fun when Alice was around. She made everything more fun. Even stupid things that shouldn't have been fun at all.

When we got home, my little sister Rosie asked if she could read the comic. She's only three, and can't read anyway, but I let her. She tore two pages and I didn't even care.

Chapter two

First day in sixth class over. My last year in National School. My eighth and last time to walk into that ugly grey building at the beginning of a new school year. My first time to walk in without Alice by my side.

It was awful. There were the usual awful things – like being the only one whose books were covered in old wallpaper instead of shiny coloured contact. And being the only one who didn't have new markers or colouring pencils. Mum made me root through our big box of colouring stuff for a set of pencils. I ended up with one of every colour, but none of them matched, and all of them were dirty-looking.

Mum didn't care. 'Everyone's pencils will be dirty in a week. And at least you won't be contributing to the piles of rubbish in our city.'

Mum has a big thing about piles of rubbish. Every time I ask for something new she says. 'You don't even need it. It'll only end up in a big pile of rubbish.'

Anyway, as well as all the usual bad things about school, there was the really, really, really bad thing of Alice not being there.

Our new teacher, Miss O'Herlihy, said we could sit wherever we liked for the first day. That was the worst part, I think. Melissa and all her buddies grabbed the seats at the back and sat there like big grinning hyenas. The boys all sat with each other as usual. The twins Ellen and Emma sat together of course, in their own exclusive little club of two. So that just left me and Jane.

Jane and I have a lot in common now. We both have no friends. Only difference is, Jane doesn't deserve them. She still tells tales, even in sixth class. And she thinks everyone except for her is 'frightfully immature.' She has her hair cut short like a boy's, and she wears a helmet when she cycles to school. I know it might save her life some day, but it's social death to be seen in a cycle helmet, and Jane doesn't even care.

We stood at the side of the room and looked at each other. I couldn't decide which was worse – sitting on my own, or sitting with Jane. In the end it didn't matter. There were only two seats left anyway, and they were together, right at the front of the class, touching Miss O'Herlihy's desk.

As I saw it, I had only two choices. I could run

away and cry, or I could sit down. I decided to be brave. I slowly walked to the top of the room, and took one of the empty seats. Jane sat next to me. She took out her Barbie pencil case and began to arrange her pens on the desk. And the pencil case wasn't even a present from a mad aunt. Jane bought it herself with her pocket money. I was sure I could hear Melissa sniggering somewhere behind me. I didn't look around.

I think it's time to tell you about Melissa.

She's beautiful, in a horrible, conceited kind of way. She has shiny blonde hair, which she never ties up. She just lets it sort of float all around her face like the princesses in my old fairy-story books. When I leave my hair loose I look like a cartoon witch.

All the teachers love Melissa. She's fooled them you see. They don't know how mean she is when they aren't around. They think she's all sweet and perfect. Considering how much time the teachers spend telling us to not to judge people by their appearance, it's a bit stupid of them to have fallen for Melissa's innocent smile, and her exquisite blonde beauty.

Melissa has a secret club. The club doesn't have any rules or any passwords or anything. They think they're too cool for that kind of thing. It's just a big group of girls who all think that Melissa is the greatest thing since water yo-yos. Mostly all they do is gather around her, and admire her hair and her trendy clothes, and laugh at her jokes.

Melissa never liked Alice and me. I don't know why. Alice didn't care. And when Alice was around, I didn't care that much either. But without Alice, all the bad things seemed worse. Every time Melissa laughed, I was sure she was laughing at me. And every time one of her friends whispered to another, I was sure they were telling awful secrets about me.

After school, I walked home on my own, missing Alice more than ever. It wasn't any fun, and for the first time ever, it felt like a very long walk.

Mum asked me how my day was, and I just said, 'fine,' even though there wasn't a single fine thing about it.

I had nothing to do after school. This was time I should have been spending with Alice. I half-wished that I had homework – at least it would have been something to do. I couldn't tell Mum that I was bored though. Whenever I did that, her reaction was the same. She'd give a huge sigh, and say that she'd love the chance to be bored. Then she'd give me a long list of horrible jobs like tidying the odd-sock drawer or dusting the skirting boards.

In the end, Mum let me go on the computer, so I checked to see if there was an e-mail from Alice.

There wasn't. She was probably too busy having fun with all her fancy new Dublin friends. She was probably planning her first sleepover party. Or drawing up a list of friends to invite to the pictures, or for a pizza. My mum said Alice's mum was a great one for 'throwing money at her problems.' No chance of my mum doing that. It wouldn't have helped anyway. Even if Mum did have a personality transplant, and gave me fifty euro to take my friends out for a treat, who would I ask? There was no one. No one at all. I'd be the sad girl, all alone in the cinema, with three boxes of popcorn and five cups of Coke and no friends.

I felt like crying then. I wondered if tears would damage the computer keyboard.

Mum came in and saw me looking at the blank screen. She rubbed my head and asked if I wanted to watch television. She even let me watch *The Simpsons*, without sighing and shaking her head every few minutes. I knew then that she must be feeling really sorry for me.

And that made me feel even worse.

Chapter three

Over the next few days, I sent Alice lots of e-mails, but they all came bouncing straight back to me like stupid, unwanted boomerangs. I didn't know why. Alice was always better with computers than I was. She would have understood. But there wasn't much point in e-mailing her to ask why my e-mails weren't getting to her, was there?

Mum said I could phone Alice instead, but only on Saturday when long-distance calls are cheaper. I wonder how come she always knows that kind of thing?

School didn't improve as the week went on. But then, I hadn't really expected it to. At twelve I was too big to believe in easy solutions.

Melissa and her buddies loved being in sixth class. They sort of sailed up and down the corridors, flicking their hair and wiggling their bottoms, and all the little kids looked up to them like they were real important.

In the yard, they sat on the benches, and tossed their hair some more, and tried their best to look cool and sophisticated. Jane spent yard time reading books about boring stuff like ancient history. Ellen and Emma walked around in their own little world, as if no-one else even existed. And all the boys played football. Even the boys who hated PE played football. I suppose it's their way of being part of the gang.

Miss O' Herlihy is nice enough. For a teacher. She smiles a lot, but for some reason even the boldest kids do what she says. She was nice to me, and talked to me in a gentle, interested kind of voice. Like she really cared. I wondered if she was sorry for me because it looked like I had no friends. Sometimes I felt like telling Miss O'Herlihy that I did have a friend, but that she moved away. Then I thought that sounded really silly, so I didn't say it. Maybe she knew anyway. Maybe the other teachers told her. Maybe not though. I bet they had more interesting stuff to talk about in the staff-room. Like where to buy cheap baked beans, and quick ways to mark maths copies and stuff.

At last Saturday morning came. At eight o' clock, I went in to Mum and Dad's room.

'Can I phone Alice now? Remember you promised?'

Dad poked his head from under the covers.

'Huh. It's a bit early, isn't it? Bet her mum isn't home yet.'

Mum kicked him under the duvet, and he didn't say any more. I knew what he meant though. Dad thinks Alice's mum goes out every night, and stays out really late going to clubs and things. Still, maybe he's just jealous, because he never goes anywhere except to work and soccer matches.

Mum gave Dad a really cross look. She smiled at me.

'No darling, don't ring just yet. They might still be in bed. Wait until half nine.'

I went back to my room and waited. It seemed like a very long time. I looked at the picture of Alice and me that I kept next to my bed. It was in a 'Best Friends' frame, that we agreed was a bit babyish, but just about cute enough not to matter. Alice had one the same. I felt sure she wasn't looking at hers. She was probably planning what to wear to a party in a new friend's house. Or wondering which of her new friends to go shopping with. Maybe she had taken my picture out of the frame and replaced it with a photo of one of her new friends. Alice wasn't disloyal by nature, but she was smart. I wasn't much good to her when I lived so far away. I couldn't blame her for trying to make new friends. The thought of that made me really sad, though.

At last half past nine came. I took the portable phone into my room, and dialled the number Alice had given me.

Alice answered after only three rings. Her voice was kind of quiet.

'Hello?'

'Hi, Al. It's me, Meg. How are you?'

'Meg!' She said it in a real excited way that made me feel happy and sad at the same time.

'Meg,' she said again. 'It's great to hear from you. How's school? What's Miss O'Herlihy like? How is Melissa? How are you?'

I laughed. Alice was always in a rush to talk. Like she had too many things to say, and not enough time to say them all.

'Well. School's awful without you. I have to sit next to Jane.'

'Ouch. Poor you.'

Then I felt a bit mean. 'Well, Jane's not so bad.

Just kind of boring you know. We don't have a whole lot in common, you know. Miss O'Herlihy's nice – for a teacher. Melissa was always awful anyway. And I feel awful.'

Alice spoke quietly. 'Yeah, I know. My school's OK. The teacher's nice. And the kids are too. But they all have their own friends, and I know they're only being nice to me because the teacher asked them to. They're kind of polite and friendly for a little while, and then they rush back to their old friends, looking kind of pleased with themselves for being so nice to the "new girl." My uniform is yuck. It's brown like your dad's car. And the material is all scratchy. And the tie is the colour of your old fish's skin before it died. And our apartment is kind of boring. It's all painted a kind of light creamy colour. Mum says it's minimalist. I think it looks as if the owner was too mean to buy much furniture. There's no garden. Just a balcony. When you stand on it all you can see is the car park. I hate it.'

I wasn't sure what I should say to that. 'Do you miss your dad?'

She gave a scornful kind of laugh. 'Course I do. Wouldn't you?'

Then I felt kind of stupid. What kind of a daft question was that?

There was a moment's silence, and then Al spoke again. 'Hey, Meg, look out quick. Is Dad's car there? He's coming up to see me today.'

I went into the front room and looked out of the window. Her dad's car was gone from its usual place.

'No, Al. It's gone.'

'Great, he's on his way so. He's taking me to the zoo. Mum took us there on Monday after school, but I don't think I should tell Dad that. He thinks it's going to be a big treat. I'll have to pretend to be really excited about it, which is a pain. The pandas stink really badly. Almost as badly as Darren Blake's football boots.'

I giggled. 'That bad?'

'Yeah. That bad. And then, after the zoo, we're going for pizza.'

'Well,' I said. 'You love pizza. So at least that'll be a treat, won't it?'

Alice sighed. 'Not really. We've had pizza three times this week already. The delivery boy knows all our names by now., and which kinds of pizzas we like. Mum says that with all the hassle from the move, she hasn't time to be cooking as well.'

'Is your dad going to stay with you tonight?'

'No. Mum said they could be civilised, and he could sleep in Jamie's room, but Dad said no. So he's staying with our Uncle John. I wish he'd stay with us.'

I wandered back into my room and lay on my bed. 'Maybe he'll stay with you next time.' I was fairly sure he wouldn't, but didn't like to say so. I changed the subject. 'Have you fixed up your e-mail yet?'

'No, but Dad's going to connect up the computer for me tonight.'

She laughed then. 'Mum tried to connect it, but she couldn't get it to work. Then she got really mad. She threw the manual on the floor after a while. And then she said all the bad words she won't let me use. Jamie copied her, and she banned him from sweets for the rest of the day. It wasn't fair on him, but I wasn't arguing, not with the mood she was in.'

I laughed. Al was always good at telling stories. I wanted to tell her that I missed her. That things were all different now that she was gone. But I thought that might have sounded kind of stupid. Only girls on the telly got away with saying that kind of thing.

So I told her about Rosie's new back tooth, and Mum's new haircut, and how Dad asked if the hairdresser was cross with her, and how they rowed for twenty minutes afterwards.

After a while, Mum tapped on the door and came into my room. She looked like she was still in a bad mood. She pointed to her watch. I held up one finger to show I wanted to talk for one more minute. She nodded and went back out.

'I have to go soon, Al. When are you coming to Limerick? Will your mum let you come down soon?'

Alice made a sad kind of sighing noise.

'I don't think so. She says after all she's paid up front for my music lessons, I'm only allowed to miss one if I'm nearly dead. I don't know if I'll ever be back again.'

I felt like crying, but that would have been too pathetic, so I very quickly said 'Bye, Al. Talk to you next week.'

Then I hung up.

I lay on my bed and looked at the ceiling. I could see the glow-in-the-dark stickers that Alice had helped me stick up. She had thought of a very clever trick using a sweeping brush and a tiny piece of Blu-Tak. Alice always had great ideas. I really missed her.

I cried for a little while, but it didn't make me

feel any better, so I got dressed and went downstairs for breakfast.

It was porridge.

As if I didn't feel quite bad enough already.

Chapter four

On Monday I got an e-mail from Alice. I was really excited. It was the first one I ever got. (Not counting all the ones I got telling me my messages to her were undelivered.) I scrolled really quickly through it, reading as fast as I could.

```
Dear Meg,
  This is my first e-mail. I
hope you get it. I had an ok
weekend. Dad took me and Jamie
lots of places. He never found
```

out that we'd been to the zoo already. I had bribed Jamie with a whole packet of Starburst, just in case. I knew it would work because as you know, Jamie would do anything for sweets. Dad was kind of sad though. Mum was kind of bubbly, and nice to Dad, but it didn't help. Actually, I think that made it worse. Yesterday when Dad was going away, Jamie was crying. I felt like crying too, but I thought that would make Dad sadder, so I pretended to be happy. Afterwards I thought he might have been a bit insulted so next week I might try a kind of brave, sad look. When Dad was gone, Mum gave Jamie and me a big bag of sweets each. I know that's what happens in films. She's trying to make it up to us because now we're kids from a broken home. She must be mad if she thinks a bag of sweets will make up for being away from home, and from Dad and from you. I'm a bit old to be so easily fooled. I don't think Jamie even fell for it. School was a bit better today. A girl called Sophie shared her crisps with me, and we chatted in the yard. Have to go now. Tea's ready. It's pizza (again!!!!). I'll ring you on Saturday.

Al xxx

I was all excited. When I'd finished reading it, I read it again a bit more slowly. Mum was nice and even stopped peeling the potatoes to show me how to reply. When she was safely back in the kitchen, this is what I wrote.

Dear Al

This is my first e-mail too. Well, the first one you might actually get. My weekend was real boring. Yesterday Dad made us go to Cratloe for a real long walk. It was pouring rain, but Dad just kept on saying "a bit of drizzle never hurt anyone, sure isn't your skin waterproof?" That really annoyed me. We went off the track and got lost. Mum got cross and said 'what if I had high heels on?' Dad laughed and said she hadn't worn high heels since the day she got married. Mum pretended to be even crosser, but I knew she wasn't. Then they got all smoochy, (yuck) and I had to wheel Rosie's buggy. That was very hard because the path was all bumpy. In the end Dad had to take over and Mum walked with me. She kept talking about feelings and stuff, so I ran after Dad and pretended I wanted to look for conkers. We didn't find any, but at least it kept Mum off my back. We had pancakes for tea (yum). School today was still awful. Melissa is as smug as ever. Can't think of any more to write. Looking forward to talking to you on Saturday.

Meg

At dinnertime, Mum kept going on to Dad about the e-mails. You'd think I'd discovered a cure for cancer or something.

'Isn't it great, Donal? Megan and Alice are e-mailing each other. Isn't that a grand way of keeping in touch? Technology's great all the same, isn't it?'

Dad just kept on nodding. I was really cross, though. What good were e-mails? I wanted a real friend. One I could see, and mess around with and laugh with. Not one who existed only on a white screen, and through a telephone. What kind of a friend was that?

I felt like shouting all that out to Mum, when she kept on about the wonders of new technology and stuff, but I didn't. I hadn't been Mum's daughter for twelve years for nothing. I knew she'd be sympathetic, but then I'd be rewarded with hours of speeches about feelings and stuff. It wasn't worth it.

So I tidied up after the dinner, and played with Rosie and waited for bedtime.

When Mum came to tuck me in, I had a great idea. 'Mum, you know how you think technology is so great?'

She looked at me suspiciously. 'Yes.'

'Well, if I had a mobile phone, I could text Alice whenever I liked. It would be a good use of technology, don't you think?'

Mum laughed. 'A good use of my money, you mean. Come on Megan. You know I don't like mobile phones. We still don't know what they do to your brain. A lot of people might be very sorry in a few years time. Very sorry indeed. I think you'd better just stick to the landline, and the computer.'

She kissed me, and went out of the room.

I snuggled under the blankets, and sighed. I love my mum, but she's such a dinosaur it's totally embarrassing. I was sure I lived in the most backward house in Ireland. If a huge volcano, like the one in Pompeii, erupted in our back garden, and covered our house with lava, it would surely fool the archaeologists in a million years time. They'd have awful trouble trying to decide when it happened.

They'd scrunch up their faces. 'Hmm. Carbon

dating says twenty-first century, and we have found a computer, but that couldn't be right.'

The others would chorus. 'No microwave oven.'

'No mobile phones.'

'No tumble drier.'

'No pizza packets.'

'No Playstation.'

'No video.'

And then they'd go home and write their papers and decide we lived in the 1950s or some ancient time like that.

It's just not fair.

Chapter five

I give out a lot about my mum. I can't help it really. All the other mums (except for Alice's of course) seem to be kinder, and easier, and just more fun. It's not fair. How come I got stuck with the crazy mum? The one who is on a permanent crusade? When all the other mums are fussing about their hair and their clothes, my mum is busy trying to save the world, or the universe. She always thinks she's right, and maybe she is, but I don't care, I just wish she'd chill out and relax a bit.

Anyway, one Friday a few weeks later, she was her usual bossy self, and it seemed that she had found yet another way to make me seem like a total loser. Then, on the Saturday, she did something which was so completely and wonderfully out of character that I thought for a while that I'd died, and been reborn into a normal family.

Anyway, this is what happened. On Friday, when I got home from school, Mum was ranting and raving because there was a piece in the paper saying that someone is planning to build a new housing estate which will take a big chunk out of the park. Her face was all red, she was so cross.

'Can you believe it, Megan? Can you?'

I shrugged. I didn't care much either way. I'm too big for parks.

'They are going to steal our park, our only

green area from us. How can we stand by and let them do this?'

She stopped and I realized that she was waiting for an answer. I made a big mistake.

'Well, you always say the park is full of druggies. You never let me go there. Wouldn't it be better if it was turned into a housing estate?'

Now Mum's face nearly went purple. She actually hit her head with her hand.

'My own daughter! What kind of a child have I raised? How can you suggest that we just concrete over our problems instead of dealing with them properly?'

I spoke in a small voice. 'I was joking, Mum.' I hadn't been joking of course, but I thought that might calm her down. She didn't even hear me though. She ran into the playroom and got one of Rosie's old paintings. On the back she drew a plan of how the park could look if the wild areas were cleared, and if a keeper was employed to maintain it and scare the druggies away. By now she had that fiery glint in her eyes that always makes me very, very nervous indeed. Then she ran to the computer and started printing out petition sheets. I started to feel sick. She was going to wave these around in public, and humiliate me one more time.

I went and stood behind her. 'Mum, you can't. I mean you wouldn't... You wouldn't go out and ask people to sign these? Would you?'

She gave me a scary kind of smile. 'No, darling. I'm not going to go out to ask people to sign these. You are.'

I argued – of course I did. I argued for a long time. But it didn't do me much good. Sometimes Mum just can't be stopped, and it's easier to give in than to argue any more. And so, some time later I found myself standing outside the local shop, clutching a clipboard.

It was the most embarrassing half hour of my entire life. A few mad old ladies came and signed in faint spidery writing. (They thought it was a petition against bin charges, and I didn't bother to explain that they were wrong.) I didn't get many signatures after that, maybe because I spent most of the time with the clipboard under my coat. Just my luck though, when I did have it out, Melissa passed by, and even though I pulled my hat down over my eyes, she still saw me and came over with a big, false show of interest. She grabbed the clipboard from me, and gave her evil, loud laugh when she saw what it was. For a moment, I considered begging her not to tell anyone at school. Then I got sense. She'd just listen to the begging and then tell everybody anyway. You can't appeal to the better nature of someone who doesn't have one. I wished that Alice was there. Alice would have known what to do. But I just stood there with a stupid big red face, saying nothing, In the end, Melissa went away, but I could hear her laughing even after she went around the corner.

I felt like crying. I wanted to go home, but I

knew Mum would kill me for having done so badly. She'd probably have insisted on coming back down with me, and started jumping around and shouting, drawing attention to us, making things even worse.

Just then, Sandra, the nice woman who works in the shop, came out. She looked at the clipboard and smiled at me. 'Has your mum asked you to do this?'

I nodded miserably.

'Why don't you leave this with me, and go for a walk for twenty minutes?'

She took the clipboard from me, and went back into the shop. I didn't know what she was at, but by then I didn't care, so I did what she said anyway. I walked ten times around the block, and when I came back, Sandra had collected three pages of signatures. I felt like hugging her, but resisted – just in case Melissa was still hanging around. Things were bad enough without being seen hugging nice shopkeepers in public.

When I got home, Mum was really pleased. She kept going on and on about how good it made her feel that I worked so hard to improve my environment, and that she felt like she was a success as a mother for having raised such a good, environmentally aware daughter, and how sorry she was for being cross with me earlier. She went on so long that I felt like throwing up. In the end her gushing did dry up, and I escaped to my room. A while later I could hear Mum on the phone in the hall. I figured she was phoning Dad to tell him the wonderful news about his daughter who was going to save the world. I turned up my radio, and drowned out Mum's voice.

Ten minutes later she tapped on the door. For a moment I felt like hiding under the bed, but I knew she'd track me down anyway, so I just sat there, and said 'come in' in as unwelcoming a voice as I could manage.

She came in and sat beside me, and put one arm around my shoulder. I braced myself for more praise, but she just said, 'Megan, you've been so good that I've decided to treat you. Dad will mind Rosie tomorrow, and you and I are going to have a great day out.'

It was hard to be enthusiastic. Mum's idea of a great day out wasn't likely to be much fun for me. She was probably going to take me to a compost-making workshop or something. Still, it was only polite to ask.

'Where are we going?'

She just gave me a huge grin and said. 'Wait and see, Megan. Just you wait and see.'

It almost sounded like a threat.

Chapter six

Next morning, Mum called me at some horribly early hour. It was dark outside, and it felt like it was still the middle of the night.

She tapped me on the shoulder. 'Come on, Megan, get up. We're going on our trip.'

I moaned and turned over. 'Aw, Mum. I'm tired. Can't we go later?' *(Or maybe never.)*

She laughed. 'No, Megan, we can't go later. Now get up and get dressed quickly, if you don't hurry we'll miss the train.'

Suddenly I didn't feel tired any more. I sat up in bed. Mum's 'special trips' usually involved walking, or bikes, or once even a canoe journey. Mention of a train was good news. Maybe we were going to visit my cousins in Mallow. Or maybe she was going to take me to Cork and buy me some vaguely fashionable clothes.

I got dressed as quickly as possible, and ate all my porridge without complaining.

When we were driving to the station, I kept asking, but Mum still wouldn't tell me where we were going, and it was only when we got to the ticket window that I heard the magic words 'An adult and a child day return to Dublin.'

I didn't dare to hope. 'Mum, could I…? I mean….. Are we…?'

She didn't answer. She spent ages putting her change in her purse, and checking that her bag was zipped up safely, and then she turned to me with a big smile. 'Are we what?'

I was so excited I could hardly get the words out. 'Are we going to see Alice?'

She shook her head and the hopes I hadn't dared to hope vanished into the cold, diesel-scented air. Then Mum continued. 'No, *we* aren't going to see Alice. But *you* are. I'm going shopping, and you get to spend the day with Alice.'

I still didn't want to hope. This had to be too good to be true. 'But.... what about her music lessons, and her dad? Isn't she spending the day with him? What if she's not even there? She might be gone out somewhere.'

Mum smiled again. She's really quite pretty when she smiles. She should do it more often. 'Don't worry, love. It's all arranged. I spoke to her mother yesterday. Alice's music lesson will be over by the time we get there, and her dad isn't going up until tomorrow. Now hurry up or we'll miss the train.'

I was so happy that I gave her a huge hug, and in my mind, I forgave her for the petition thing the day before. I didn't tell her that, though, I didn't want her getting ideas.

The train journey seemed to take forever. Mum proved that she hadn't totally lost it, so instead of tea and chocolate muffins, I got a healthy snack of sunflower seeds and organic apple juice. I didn't care though.

Next we got a taxi to Alice's new apartment. I rang the buzzer, and could hardly stop myself from jumping up and down while I waited for an answer. Then I heard Alice's voice. 'Who is it?' It was funny talking to a metal box. 'It's me. I mean, Megan.'

She laughed. 'Well, come on in. It's the second floor.' There was a clicking noise, and the door opened. Mum kissed me goodbye, and promised to be back to collect me at half past four. I looked at my watch. That was five and a half hours. Heaven. Then I ran up the stairs as fast as if there was a whole crowd of mad park-petitioners after me.

Alice met me halfway up. We both stopped. I felt shy, which was really stupid, since I was only meeting my very best friend in the whole world who I hadn't seen for five long weeks. She looked kind of shy as well, so I didn't feel too bad. Then her mum's voice floated down the stairs. 'Alice O'Rourke, were you by any chance born in a field? Get up here and close that door.'

We both laughed, and all of a sudden everything was OK. Alice put her arm over my shoulder. 'Come on up, Megan. Welcome to my new life.'

When we got into the apartment, Alice's mum came out into the hallway and shook my hand. 'Why, hello Megan. How very nice to see you.' She didn't look like she meant it. As usual she was dressed like a model, all slinky clothes and high-heeled pointy boots.

Then Jamie came over. He looked smaller than I remembered. 'Did you bring sweets?' I shook my head, and he immediately lost interest in me. Alice's mum put on her coat, and bullied Jamie into his. 'Now, Alice. You know I'm trusting you, so you have to be on your best behaviour. I've left you some sandwiches in the fridge. I'll be back at five.'

Then with a click-click of her very high heels she was gone. I could hardly believe it. I grinned at Alice and she grinned at me. Then she took me by the hand and pulled me into her bedroom. She lay on her bed, and I sat on a huge purple bean-bag, and we said all the silly things we hadn't been able to say for weeks. She laughed at all my funny stories about Melissa, and she made a face when I told her about the petition the day before.

Then she told me about her school. It sounded just like any other school – pretty boring. Then I noticed that she looked really sad.

'What's wrong, Al? Is it awful?'

She shook her head. 'Not really. The teachers are OK. And some of the girls are quite nice. It's just that I keep wishing that I was back in Limerick, that's all. I miss Dad. I miss you. Sometimes I think I even miss Melissa.'

I didn't know what to say. Alice was usually so positive, I didn't know how to cope with this new, sad girl.

Then she shook her head like she was trying to push away all the bad thoughts. She jumped up and smiled. 'Anyway, enough moaning. Let's go out for something to eat.'

I was shocked. I'd never been out to eat without an adult before. 'But didn't your mum say she's left us some food?'

Alice laughed. 'Oh, yeah, that. Let's check it out.' She led me back into the kitchen, and pulled open the fridge door. She took out a plate covered in foil. She peeled back the foil and revealed a stack of small white sandwiches with the crusts cut off. She put her nose down and sniffed. 'Yuck! Tuna. I'm not eating these.'

I actually quite like tuna sandwiches, especially when I don't have to eat the crusts, but I didn't like to say so.

She threw them into the bin, and covered them up with an old newspaper. Then she grabbed her coat and led me to the hallway. 'Come on, Megan. It's time for your tour.'

We had a lovely few hours. We went to a fast food restaurant and had a giant bag of chips. Then we bought a monster ice-cream each. Then we hung around a shopping centre, looking at the clothes and the CDs and the jewellery. We bumped into a girl from Alice's class, Janine, and we chatted for a few minutes. She seemed nice and friendly, but I felt so jealous it gave me a pain in my head. I couldn't bear the thought of Alice having a best friend who wasn't me. When she'd gone, I tried to act casual. 'Do you like her?'

Alice thought for a moment. 'Yeah. She's nice.'

It was like a knife twisting in my heart. Then Alice continued. 'But she's not half as nice as you.' I felt a lot better then.

After that, we went for a walk, and got more chips and then it was four o'clock.

We went back to Alice's apartment. Alice rooted around the kitchen and found some chocolate biscuits. We took them into her room, but I didn't feel like eating them. I felt kind of sick after all the chips. I sat on the beanbag again, and played with the zip of my jacket. I didn't want to go home. I didn't want to leave Alice behind in this place that wasn't home. She was very quiet. She was looking out the window with her shoulders all sort of hunched over. I went over and stood beside her. There was no garden outside – just an ugly old car park. I felt like crying, but that would have been really mean. Alice had much more reason to cry than I had.

She made a sudden kind of a croaky noise. I felt sick. I hadn't seen Alice cry since she was about six. I wondered if I should hug her. Then I looked at her, and saw that she wasn't crying. She was laughing. As I watched, she turned to me and laughed out loud. For a minute I thought that she had gone completely mad. She looked like she had completely lost it.

'What is it, Al? What's so funny?'

'I'll tell you what's so funny, Megan. I've just had the most wonderful idea ever. I have a plan.'

'What kind of plan?'

She laughed again. 'A plan to put an end to all this. A plan so you and I can be together again.'

Now I knew she'd gone mad. Nothing would persuade her mother to move back to Limerick. I felt sorry for Alice again. She'd have to tell me about her plan, and I'd have to be the one to tell her all the reasons it wouldn't work. Sometimes, being the sensible one in a friendship was very hard work.

I sighed. 'So tell me about your plan.'

She shook her head. 'No, I won't. You'll only tell me it won't work.'

I went red, but she didn't seem to notice. She went on talking. 'But it will work, I promise. I just have to work out a few details.'

Now I was interested. 'Please, Al, tell me.'

She shook her head. 'No, Meg. Sorry. Just trust me for once. I'll tell you when I see you again.'

'But when will that be? I know Mum won't bring me up here again.'

She shrugged. 'Well, sometime soon, Mum will have to let me go to Limerick. Don't worry, I'll see you soon, and everything will be fine, I promise. All will be revealed the next time I see you.'

Alice was good at keeping secrets. I knew there was no point in pushing her. And also, I knew that underneath all her laughing and joking, she really was very unhappy. She missed her dad, and she missed her old life. She was my best friend, and it was my duty to help her. I had a funny feeling that however mad or crazy her plan was, I'd end up helping her to put it into action.

Just then, I saw a taxi pulling up outside. Mum got out and walked to the entrance of the apartment building. The buzzer in the hall went. Alice walked me downstairs. She chatted to Mum for a minute, and then winked at me when Mum wasn't looking. Then Mum checked her watch. 'Sorry, girls, but we have to go. I don't want to miss the train.'

Alice and I had a quick hug, and then I got into the taxi with Mum. I looked back as we drove off. Alice was still grinning madly, and for one precious minute, I really believed that she could fix everything.

Chapter seven

It was strange going back to school on Monday. Everything was just like before, and it was kind of like the weekend had never happened. I wanted to tell someone about my trip to Dublin, but the only person I could think of was Miss O'Herlihy, and telling the teacher was too sad for words. So I didn't tell anyone.

Melissa had sprained her arm on Saturday, and everyone was fussing over her so much that she didn't get a chance to tease me about the petition. Fingers crossed, I thought, with any luck she'll forget about it altogether.

* * *

And so a few weeks went by, boring, just like before. As usual, Alice e-mailed me every few days. I wanted to send her a message every day but Mum wouldn't let me. She said that would make me seem desperate. I was desperate of course, but I couldn't tell Mum that. She'd only have started one of those serious talks I hated. And I couldn't sneak a message without Mum knowing because she won't tell me the password for the computer. She thinks the Internet is a dangerous place for kids. When she said that, Dad said the world is a dangerous place anyway and why not just lock me up in an ivory tower altogether and be done with it. Then Mum gave Dad one of her not-in-front-of-the-children looks and that was the end of that.

Alice and I took turns to phone each other on

Saturdays. I never had much to say. Alice always had lots. She was making friends. She mentioned Janine a few times. Even though I was glad for Alice, I couldn't help feeling a bit jealous too. Sometimes she mentioned her secret plan, but I pretended not to be interested, even though I was dying with curiosity.

Then, just before Halloween, I got the e-mail I was waiting for.

Dear Meg,

The best news ever ever ever!!!!!! I'm coming home at Halloween. Jamie can't come because he has a soccer match (yippee!) so it will be just me and Dad. I'll be coming down on the train. And I can see you every day. It'll be fantastic. Mum says I can stay for three days. She said it would be unsettling to stay for longer than that... I didn't argue too much, because of THE PLAN. I can't say any more in case anyone else reads this. Does your mum read your messages? Mine doesn't, but that's only because she still can't work the computer. (Let's hope she never learns.) Anyway, I'll e-mail you again soon, and I'll see you in sixteen days. I can't wait.

Al xxxxxx

Those sixteen days were very long. It felt more like sixteen hundred days. Every night I crossed off another day on the calendar over my desk in my bedroom. Mum said that wouldn't make them go any faster, and she was right, but I continued anyway. I hadn't anything else to do.

At last it was the Friday of mid-term. I was so happy, I felt like shouting and screaming and dancing out of school. (Of course I didn't do it. Melissa and her buddies would never ever let me forget something like that.) Even so, I found myself giving an odd little skip every now and then as I walked home.

When I got home I changed out of my uniform, and hung it in the wardrobe, shoving it right to the back. After all, I wouldn't be wearing it again for ten more wonderful, happy, Melissa-free days. I put on my best jeans and the top Mum bought me on the day Alice had left. Then I sat in my room and waited. I tried to read my new Jacqueline Wilson book, but I couldn't concentrate. I was reading the words and turning the pages, but I had no idea what was happening in the story.

It was a long wait. It was nearly six o'clock before I heard Alice's dad's car stopping outside. I ran out to the front door. Alice was just getting out of the car. I hadn't seen her for five whole weeks. She looked just the same. She had a new denim jacket, and great new jeans.

'Meg!' she shouted, when she saw me, and she ran over to me. We even hugged.

Her dad smiled. 'Oh, hello, Megan. I see you two are glad to see each other. Would you like to come inside with Alice for a while?'

I knew Mum would give out to me later for 'invading their privacy', but I didn't care.

'I'd love to thanks,' I said. Alice put her arm around me and we went inside.

It was funny being in her house again. I'd spent half my life there before, but hadn't been in there since Al had left. It was tidy, but it was very cold. Al's dad went upstairs with her bag, and Al and I went into the family room. All of Al's books were still on the shelf, and Jamie's toys were in the corner where they always used to be. They used to have a fancy black and white family photograph hanging over the fireplace, but it was gone.

I sat on the beanbag, and Al lay on the leather

couch. With her shoes on. She noticed me looking at her feet.

'That's one of the good things about being from a broken home. There's different rules. Mum would kill me for putting my feet on the couch, but Dad doesn't care. And in Dublin, I can leave doors open, and lights on, because they're the things Dad hates, so Mum just lets me do them. She doesn't care, as long as I don't mess the place up, or make too much noise.'

I laughed. Even being in the same room as Al again made me feel good. There were loads of things I wanted to tell her, but first there was the one big thing I had to ask. I took a deep breath. 'Come on, Al. Now's the time. What's your secret plan? How are you going to get us back together again?'

She looked towards the door, and whispered. 'I'm not going back to Dublin on Monday.'

I was so delighted that I forgot all about the plan. 'Hey, that's great. Are you staying for the whole week? Your dad must be pleased. But how did you get your mum to change her mind?'

Al put on one of the mysterious looks that I knew so well.

'She didn't change her mind. That's the plan. She thinks I'm going back, but I'm not.'

Alice was my best friend, but even I had to admit that she sometimes had crazy ideas. She kind of got all excited, and forgot that she was living in the real world, not a nice, easy, story-book kind of world. She always thought life could be like the movies.

I looked at her. She was lying back on the couch, like she was all relaxed, but her eyes had that wild, crazy kind of sparkle, that always made me a little bit afraid.

I had to ask. 'But won't your dad just make you go back?'

She smiled. 'Well, actually, he won't know any-thing about it.'

I tried not to sound too suspicious. 'How

exactly are you going to fix that?'

She gave me a big grin. 'Easy. You're going to help me.'

I smiled nervously. Nothing was ever as easy as Alice thought it would be. Still though, I didn't really care. It was great to have her back, and if she had a way to stay for longer than three days, I was all for it.

Just then, the doorbell rang. It was Rosie, looking all cute in her dalmatian dressing-gown and pink furry slippers.

'Meggy. Home,' she said, looking very pleased with herself.

I sighed. 'Sorry, Al. I know there's no point arguing with Mum. I have to go. And I know she won't let me back after tea. She'll just say you need "quality time" with your dad. I know she won't let me out again. Will your dad let you call over do you think?'

She grimaced. 'I don't think so. He wants us to have pizza together. And I'm really starting to hate pizza. And he's rented a movie. I saw it ages ago, with Mum, but I can't tell him that, can I? I'll have to see you in the morning.'

Just then her dad appeared in the hall, so I couldn't ask any more about Al's big plan. She was probably very pleased about that. She loved dragging things out, keeping me in suspense.

Her dad had the phone in his hand. 'Sorry for interrupting girls, I'm just going to order the pizza. Pepperoni for you, Alice?'

Alice made a face behind his back, and put her finger in her mouth, pretending to be sick. 'Sounds great,' she said. 'Just what I want.'

I had to run out the door so her dad wouldn't see me laughing. I just gave a little wave, behind my back, and went home to my organic pasta.

Chapter eight

Next morning I woke real early, and I got dressed straightaway. No point though, because of course Mum wouldn't let me go next door. She was afraid Alice and her dad wouldn't be up yet.

She suggested what she thought was a great idea.

'Why don't you do all your jobs now, so later, when Alice is up, you'll be free to play with her?'

(I was twelve years old. Didn't she know that twelve-year-olds don't play? Twelve-year-olds just hang out.)

So I spent an hour hoovering, and dusting, and helping Mum clean out the utility room. Every now and then I had a little grumble.

'No one else has to do as many jobs as I do. Melissa doesn't do a single thing.'

Mum had her usual answer. 'Well, I'm not Melissa's mum, am I? I can't help it if she's allowed to be a spoiled brat. And anyway, since when do you care about Melissa?'

I shrugged. 'I don't. It's just that I seem to do more jobs than anyone I know. It's not fair.'

Mum put on her serious voice then. 'I know love. It doesn't seem fair. But I don't want you thinking that the house tidies itself. It doesn't, you know. I have so much to do, and if you don't help, I'll never get through it.'

I looked at her. She did look a bit tired. So I worked even harder, jumping whenever she asked me to bring something upstairs, or to put something in the bin. By half past nine, the house looked perfect to me.

Mum sighed. 'Now for the hall cupboard.'

I groaned and Mum gave a big laugh. 'Just kidding. The hall cupboard will wait. You go and call for Alice.'

She gave me a hug, and a kiss on the cheek. 'And thanks for all your help.' I pretended to wipe the kiss away with the sleeve of my fleece, but I was pleased.

Alice opened the door as I approached her doorstep, as if she'd been waiting for me. 'At last. I've been up for hours. Dad wouldn't let me over. He said it was too early.'

'Yeah. Me too. And I've had to do loads of jobs for Mum. You'd think the president was coming to visit.'

'Well, it was worse for me. After breakfast, Dad made me look at old photographs with him. And he got all sad whenever he came to ones of the four of us. His voice kept going all funny, and I thought he was going to cry.'

'Oh no. Gross! What did you do?'

She giggled. 'I gave him a speech I heard on telly last week. I said I wanted to be positive, and look ahead, and all that old stuff. So we played Boggle instead. It was boring, but it was worth it. It's awful you know. Mum and Dad are the grown-ups, but I spend all my time minding them, as if they were the children. I have to be careful all the time. If I'm happy, it's as if I don't care that they've separated. And if I'm sad, they go all guilty on me.'

For the first time, I had kind of an idea what it must be like for her.

'Oh, I'm sorry, Al. Is it awful?'

She nodded. Then she brightened suddenly. 'Come on upstairs. We have to talk.'

We went upstairs to her bedroom. It was really untidy, as usual, with clothes strewn everywhere. Around her bedhead there was a string of pale pink flowery lights. They looked really cool.

Alice saw me looking at them. 'Dad got them for me. He keeps buying me stuff. It's the guilt thing again. I'd prefer if things were back the way they used to be though. I could live without these lights.'

I felt the petals. They were made of a shimmery, pearly kind of plastic, and were really pretty. Like something in a rich kid's house.

'You can borrow them if you like – when I'm not here,' offered Alice.

I sighed. 'Thanks, but no thanks. You know what my mum's like. She'd just say they were a waste of electricity, so she wouldn't let me plug them in. There'd be no point.'

Alice imitated my mum's voice. 'Girls, don't you know anything about global warming? What do they teach you at school these days?'

I giggled. Alice was a very good mimic.

I sat on her new blow-up chair. 'Now. I'm fed up of waiting. Tell me your plan.'

Alice threw herself onto her bed, and wriggled in excitement. 'It's one of my best. It's a classic. Simple, but effective.'

She looked at me intently. 'Simple is always the best. Then there's less to go wrong.'

I was impatient. 'Cut the waffle, and tell me. What's your plan?'

She smiled. 'Well, you see, I'm going to pretend to go back to Dublin, but I won't. Dad will think I'm with Mum, and Mum will think I'm with Dad. Like I said, it's simple. They'll ....'

I interrupted her. 'Yeah, but if you're not with your mum, and not with your dad, where exactly *will* you be?'

'That's the great part. I'll be staying in your house.'

My heart sank. Here was the big flaw I'd been afraid of. This plan could never work. I decided it was best to tell Alice now, before she got too excited. 'Sounds like fun, but my mum and dad will never agree to let you stay. Not if your parents don't know. You know how parents always stick together. It's like they have some secret code of honour or something.'

Alice laughed. 'That's the best thing of all. That's what makes this plan so brilliant. Your mum won't know I'm there. I'll be in hiding. I'll be like a hostage. I'll sneak into your room, and no one will know, except for us.'

Already I could see all kinds of problems, but then I suppose that was the difference between me and Alice. I always saw problems where she saw opportunities. 'How long do you think we'll get away with this? Until you're eighteen?'

Alice shook her head impatiently. 'Of course not. I'm not a complete dork you know! Dad will go up to Dublin on Friday to visit me, and I won't be there.'

That sounded like real trouble. 'They'll go crazy.'

Alice was unconcerned. 'Well, I suppose they'll panic a bit. That's the whole point.'

'And then?'

'And then, before they get really scared, and before they get time to call the guards, I'll ring and tell them I'm safe, and they'll be all happy and relieved.'

I thought I could see where all this was leading. 'And then they'll get back together, and the four of you can live happily ever after? I'm sorry Al, but I don't think it'll be that easy. I think you've watched *The Parent Trap* once too often.'

Alice shook her head. 'Did I mention the fact that I'm not a complete dork? I know that won't happen. That would never happen. But if Mum finally sees how upset I am about the move, she might just feel sorry enough for me to move back to Limerick. It's not like she's got a job or anything in Dublin. She could easily come back here. She could move into one of the new apartments around the corner, and I could go back and forth between her and Dad whenever I liked. It could be almost as good as before. Maybe even better. I wouldn't have to listen to Mum and Dad fighting all the time. And I could go back to school with you. And we could do stuff after school. It would be the best thing ever.'

She gave me a huge smile, and all of a sudden the whole thing seemed wonderful, and fantastic and not at all impossible.

Chapter nine

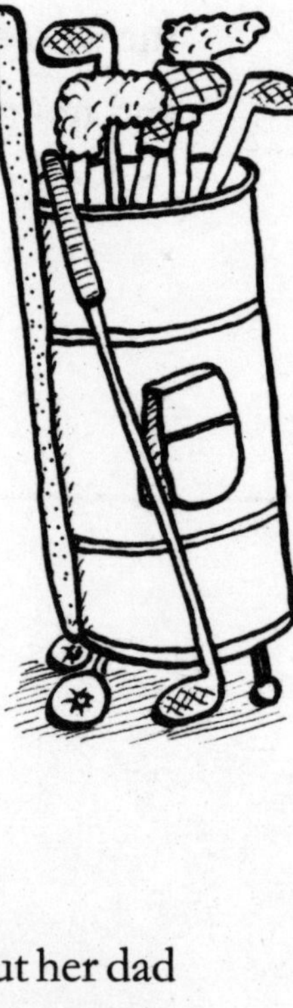

Step one of the big plan was to make sure Alice's dad wasn't around on Monday afternoon, when she was supposed to be catching the train back to Dublin. That was easy. We approached him after lunch on Sunday, when he was relaxing in their living room with the papers.

Alice kind of sidled up behind him, and sat on the arm of his chair. She put on her sweetest voice. I thought it sounded a bit over the top, but her dad didn't seem to notice. 'Dad, are you playing golf this weekend?'

He smiled at her. 'No love. I want to spend time

with you, since I see so little of you these days.'

'But Dad, I don't mind, honestly. I know how much you love playing golf. Isn't there a competition on tomorrow afternoon?'

We knew already that there was. We'd checked it in the local paper.

Alice's dad sat up, and began to look interested. 'Well, now you mention it, there is actually. I could…'

He hesitated. 'No, I couldn't. How would I get you to the station?'

Now it was my turn. My voice was even sweeter than Alice's. 'My dad has already offered. He has to pick up some things from his office tomorrow evening. It wouldn't be any trouble. He says it's fine.'

Alice's dad looked closely at me. I opened my eyes wide and tried to look innocent. I'd never be as pretty as Melissa, but luckily I was blessed with the kind of face that adults seemed to trust. I smiled my best smile.

It worked. He looked at Alice again. 'And you're sure you don't mind?'

She smiled at him. 'Quite sure.'

He thought for a moment. 'You know, you're two very considerate girls. I haven't played golf for weeks. It would be good to get out to hit a few balls. I'll just run next door, and thank your dad, Megan.'

He got up and went towards the door.

I had to think fast. 'No, don't. It's fine. He's busy. He's very busy actually. He's em, em…. He's changing Rosie's nappy.'

Alice added. 'She's got terrible diarrhoea. It's not a pretty sight, I promise. And the smell! Think really really gross, and then double it. It's like………'

I gave Alice a funny look. She was getting carried away as usual. She stopped talking and I continued. 'It just isn't very nice, believe me.'

Her dad sat down again. Luckily he didn't know that Rosie hadn't worn a nappy for at least a year. 'Oh, fine so. I'll thank him the next time I see him. Alice, get me the phone, won't you? I must ring up and book a tee-time.'

Alice got him the phone, and then we ran upstairs. We gave a quiet cheer and a high-five. Success! Step one was done and dusted.

* * *

Next day, I stood in my front garden and watched Alice hugging her dad, as he was leaving for golf.

'See you Friday, love. Only four days. Isn't that nice? Tell your mother I'll be there around seven.'

She beamed at him. 'Yeah Dad. I will. Only four days. Great.'

He gave her one more hug, then he checked his watch, and jumped into the car. He wound down the window, and looked at me. 'You're sure it's OK with your mum and dad? Should I go in and talk to them?'

Alice put on her exasperated voice. 'Dad, relax. Take a chill-pill or something. I'm spending the afternoon with Megan. I've already brought my stuff into her house, and her dad will drive me to the station at five o'clock. It's all sorted. Now go and play your golf before it's too late. Love you.'

She leaned in and kissed his cheek, and then he drove off.

It was a lovely afternoon. We spent a lot of time playing basketball shots, and chatting, just like in the old days. It was a nice feeling, knowing that we were going to be together so much for the next few days.

At five o'clock, we went into the sunroom of our house. Dad was dozing, Rosie was playing with her dolls on the floor, and Mum was reading the paper. 'Alice has come to say goodbye, Mum. She has to go now.'

Mum looked up from her paper. 'Oh dear. The weekend went so quickly, didn't it? Long weekends are never quite long enough, are they?' She went to get up. 'I'll wave you off.'

Oh no. How could I get her to stay inside? If she went out she'd see that Alice's dad's car wasn't there, and everything would be ruined. Sudden drastic action was called for. I did a very mean thing. I leaned down and gave Rosie a quick, hard pinch on the shoulder. Her reaction was immediate. She gave a huge howl, and tears began to pour down her puckered-up face. I mentally promised to give her some sweets later to make up for being so mean. Alice took her chance. 'I'll go so. Dad's waiting. Bye everybody.'

Mum was so busy consoling Rosie that all thoughts of following us were gone.

We went out the front door. We stayed outside for about ten minutes, then I went back in. Rosie was happy again, though she did give me a funny kind of look. Dad was still asleep, and Mum was engrossed in the paper.

'I'm going to my room for a while,' I said.

Mum looked up. I put on a sad face, and she gave me a sympathetic smile. 'Oh, OK dear. I'll call you when it's time for tea. It's pancakes.'

I went to my room. Luckily, I slept downstairs, in what used to be the garage. I even had my own little shower room, right next door. It was a perfect set-up for hiding friends, though I'm sure that's not what Mum and Dad had in mind when they allowed me to move down there.

I opened the bedroom window, and gave a low whistle, the special signal we had agreed earlier. Alice appeared from the bushes at the side of the house, carrying her weekend bag, and the sleeping bag we'd borrowed from her house. She climbed in, and we hid her stuff in the wardrobe. Then we sat on the bed and giggled quietly for a while. I was excited and happy and afraid all at once.

Soon Mum came to call me for tea. Luckily, I'd insisted for the past year that she and Dad knock before coming into my room, explaining that at the age of twelve, I needed some privacy. So when Mum tapped on the door, Alice had plenty of time to roll under the bed, out of sight. It worked fine – but then it should have – she'd practised about a hundred times already.

I ate my tea as quickly as possible, and went back to my room. Poor Alice wasn't happy. 'Oh, Meg. Those pancakes smelled so good. Couldn't you even get me a small scrap?'

I shook my head. 'Sorry, Al. No point taking foolish chances. How could I explain if I was caught sneaking pancakes into my room? Mum never allows me to eat in here.'

She sighed. 'Yeah, I suppose you're right.'

I smiled at her. 'Anyway, don't worry, we've got loads of food.'

I went to my wardrobe and pulled out the bag we'd been filling ever since we'd started to plan. Alice looked inside.

'Hmm. Apples or bananas or biscuits or cream crackers. I don't know where to begin.'

Suddenly all the carefully stashed food looked a bit pathetic, and I felt a bit guilty at the thought of the seven yummy, golden, buttery, lemony pancakes I'd just scoffed.

I spoke encouragingly. 'Don't worry, Al. This is just for tonight. We'll get better stuff tomorrow.'

She shrugged, and bit into an apple. 'Doesn't matter, I can be brave. And it'll all be worth it in the end. You'll see.'

Chapter ten

I went into the living room at eight o'clock that evening. Mum looked up from patching Rosie's pyjamas. Surely I lived in the only family in Ireland where the kids were expected to wear patched pyjamas. I couldn't help commenting, even though I knew Mum wouldn't pay much attention to my opinion.

'Mum, we're not poor. Dad has a good job. Can't you just buy Rosie some new pyjamas? They have lovely ones in Dunnes Stores and they cost less than ten euro.'

Mum sighed. 'Megan, how many times do I have to tell you? It's not about the money. It's about the environment. I can't in conscience throw these pyjamas in the bin just because they're a bit worn at the knees.'

Dad looked up and laughed. 'A bit worn? Actually, Sheila, they're transparent.'

Mum gave him a really filthy look, and he stopped laughing. I was sorry I'd started the whole thing. I spoke as brightly as I could. 'Actually, I just came in to say I'm going to bed.'

Mum put down her sewing and felt my forehead. 'Aren't you well, love? It's not like you to volunteer to go to bed. Especially when you've no school tomorrow.'

I tried to put on a tired smile. 'I'm fine, Mum, really. I'm just wrecked. I mustn't have slept well last night. I might read for a little while.'

Mum still looked puzzled, but she just said, 'OK so, love. Goodnight. Don't forget to brush your teeth. I'll be in in a while to tuck you in.'

I knew there was no point in arguing. I figured that if I was twenty, Mum would still have to tuck me in at night. I'd be coming home from discos at three in the morning, and Mum would be there in her dressing gown and slippers, waiting to tuck me in.

Alice would just have to be ready to hide when she came.

I kissed Dad, and skipped off to my room. So far, so good.

I changed into my pyjamas, and went into the bathroom next to my room, and locked the door. I opened the window, and gave the whistle signal. Then Alice climbed out through my bedroom window, and in the bathroom window. I climbed out of the bathroom window, and hung around in the garden until Alice was finished. It was very cold. I decided that the next night I'd stay in my clothes for that part. Then Alice climbed out of the bathroom window, and I climbed in. I went to the toilet, did my teeth and washed my face and hands. Then I unlocked the bathroom door, and sauntered back down the hallway to my room.

Alice was waiting for me, lying in her sleeping bag on the floor next to my bed. She laughed quietly. "Whew. That was kind of complicated, wasn't it? We're going to be very good at climbing by Friday. We'll be ready to tackle Mount Everest."

I laughed too. 'Just be glad I don't sleep upstairs.'

She sighed. 'Yeah, I suppose. Still, are you sure I couldn't chance just running along the hall to the bathroom?'

I shook my head. 'No way. We're not taking any chances. And I'm not risking you bumping into Mum or Dad. I want this to work.'

It was true. Although I'd been a bit doubtful at first, I was sure by then that Alice had devised a brilliant plan. It had to work. It just had to. All I could think of was having Alice back in Limerick for good. As soon as possible. I wanted us to be in the same class again. I wanted us to make our confirmation on the same day. I wanted us to go to the same secondary school, and still be best friends when we were really old – like seventeen or eighteen or something. And if I had to spend a few days climbing in and out of windows to achieve that, well it seemed to me that was a small price to pay.

Alice looked at her watch and panicked suddenly. 'Oh no, it's time to ring Mum. This is the hardest part, I know. What'll we do if she doesn't believe me?'

I tried to sound confident. 'Of course she'll believe you. Why wouldn't she? It'll be fine, I promise.'

I was a bit worried though. Alice was always the chief planner, and if she got scared, I wasn't sure I could keep things going for long.

Alice looked at me doubtfully as she took out

her mobile phone. Then, still in her sleeping bag, she wriggled onto my bed like a giant purple and pink snake. She settled herself on one of my pillows, and dialled her mum's number.

I put my ear next to hers so I could hear both sides of the conversation.

'Hi Mum. It's me, Alice.'

'Oh, hello, dear. I was just getting ready to go to the station to pick you up. Is the train on time?'

'Well, actually, I'm not on the train. I'm feeling a bit sick, so Dad said I could stay here in Limerick.'

Her mum sounded rather impatient.

'Sick? What's wrong? Wasn't Daddy minding you properly? Did he let you catch cold? Isn't that just typical!'

Alice spoke in a soothing kind of voice, like the one my mum uses with Rosie. 'No, Mum. It's not Dad's fault. I have a bit of a tummy bug, that's all, and I couldn't face the train.'

Her mother gave a long sigh. 'OK. Not much we can do now anyway, is there? I suppose there are no more trains tonight. Can you put Daddy on please?'

Alice hesitated. 'Well, actually, I can't right now. He went out.'

Now her mum sounded really cross. 'Out? Out where? How could he leave you on your own when you're sick? What on earth is that foolish man thinking of?'

'Look, Mum, I'm not going to die, you know. I'm not all that sick. Just too sick to travel. And Dad's been minding me really well all weekend, so I insisted that he go out for a while.'

There was another long sigh from the Dublin end of the phone line. 'OK. I'll see you tomorrow then. Ring me and let me know what train you're on.'

This was the hard part. I held my breath while I waited for Alice to reply.

'Well, actually, I might still be too sick to travel then. I think I'll just stay in bed for the day tomorrow. Megan's mum said she'd keep an eye on me while Dad's at work.'

There was a brief silence, and when Alice's mum spoke again, her voice scored very highly on the crossometer. 'Well, isn't that just typical of your dad, landing you in with strangers while he swans off into work? I'm sure Megan's mum has more to do than keeping an eye on you. We'll have to ...'

Alice suddenly grinned at me. 'Oh, Mum, I think I'm going to throw up. Gotta go. I'll call you tomorrow.' She made a gross, burpy sound into the phone, and then clicked it off. Then she tossed the phone carelessly onto the bed.

I looked at her admiringly. 'Wow, you're such a good liar. I wish I was as good as you.'

She gave a smug little smile. 'It's easy. All you need is lots and lots of practice. Come on, Meg, you try it, tell me a lie.'

I thought for a moment. 'Em.... Oh, I know – Melissa's the nicest girl I ever met.'

Alice gave me a disappointed look. 'No. I'm

not convinced. Try a real lie, but one I might actually believe.'

I thought again. 'OK. How about this? Rosie is a secret genius. I'm the only person in the world who knows that she can speak five languages, and play the guitar better than Bono.'

Now Alice looked really disappointed. 'Well of course I know that's a lie. Bono doesn't play guitar, he just prances around in his sunglasses and sings really cool songs.'

I was a bit annoyed. 'Well, you don't know that do you? Maybe he's the best guitarist in the world. Maybe he just plays for his family.'

Alice was getting cross. 'That's stupid. Just face it, you're wrong. He doesn't play guitar.'

I felt like arguing, but then I got sense. After all, who really cared whether Bono could play guitar or not? And besides, if Alice was going to be hiding in my room for the next four nights, it would be easier if we weren't fighting all the time. She looked at me and smiled. I had a funny feeling she was thinking the same as me.

'Sorry, Meg. Forget it. Let's play "Things we hate about Melissa." You go first.'

I grinned. That was my favourite game, and I was very good at it. 'OK. I really, really hate the way she nods all the time when the teacher is speaking, as if she knew everything already.'

'Oh, yeah. Good one. Now my turn. I really, really hate the way when she puts on her coat, she flicks her hair up, and then checks to see if anyone was watching.'

An hour passed very quickly like that, and then Alice picked up her phone again. This time she dialled her dad's number.

He picked up straightaway. 'Hello.'

He sounded kind of lonely, but maybe I was just imagining that.

'Hi, Dad. It's me, Alice.'

'Oh, hello, darling. Are you home already?'

'Yes, Dad. Safe and sound. I had a lovely weekend thanks. How was your golf?'

He sighed. 'Oh, you know. Good, but not good enough.'

I laughed quietly to myself. He always said that.

Alice was more sympathetic. 'Oh, I'm sorry.'

They had some cutie, dreadfully boring father-daughter chat for a few minutes, and then he said, 'Put me on to your mother for a minute, won't you?'

Alice was ready for that. 'I can't, Dad, sorry. She's had to go out for a while. I'm minding Jamie.'

Big mistake. 'Oh, OK. Put Jamie on, so.'

Alice was very quick. 'Oh Dad, I'm sorry. He's just gone off to sleep. I'll kiss him for you, shall I?'

Alice wouldn't have kissed her brother unless she was paid an awful lot of money, but luckily her dad didn't think of that.

'That's sweet, Allie. Kiss his cute little nose for me, won't you?'

Alice made a face at me. 'Sure, Dad.'

'Thanks, love. Look, I'd better go. So I'll see

you next Friday, OK?'

Alice gave a huge smile. 'Yes, Dad, I'll see you on Friday.'

She clicked off the phone and continued. '....and by then, my life will be changing. For the better.'

We gave each other another high five, and a big hug.

Alice beamed. 'Step two executed, and successful. We're on our way.'

Chapter eleven

I couldn't relax properly that night until Mum had been in for the tucking-in scenario she loved so much. Actually, I usually loved it too – it made me feel all cosy and safe, like when I was a little girl. But this night was different. I just wanted it over and done with so Al and I could relax and settle down for our first night together.

Alice lay on the floor next to my bed, and we conversed in whispers until, finally, there was a light tap on the door. Alice rolled expertly under the bed, taking her sleeping bag with her.

'Come in,' I said, feeling a bit like one of the three little pigs inviting the big bad wolf into his house.

Mum opened the door and came in. She sat on the edge of my bed. A bad sign. This wasn't going to be a quick kiss and a pat on the head. This was going to be serious.

She put her hand lightly on my shoulder. 'Feeling a bit better now?'

'Mmmm.'

'It's hard, Alice being gone, isn't it? You must miss her an awful lot.'

'Mmmmm.' I couldn't think of anything else to say. Whatever would my mum have said if she knew that Alice was lying only a few inches away from her, inhaling the dust from under my bed, and listening to every word Mum said?

Mum kind of rustled her behind, as if she was settling in.

'You know, Megan, something a bit like this

happened me when I was your age.'

I tried not to look bored. Either my mum was a dreadful liar, or everything that ever happened to me seemed to have happened to her at some stage too.

Mum put on her dreamy kind of voice. 'And guess what?'

I spoke in a sing-song voice. 'I bet it all turned out for the best in the end.'

Mum looked a bit hurt, so I had to add, 'I know, Mum. Thanks for trying to help.'

She smiled and patted my shoulder. 'That's OK. You know we can always talk, don't you?'

She got up to go. At the same awful moment, our eyes fell on a red sweatshirt that was neatly folded on the end of my bed. Mum picked it up, and shook it out.

'What's this? Isn't this Alice's?'

I tried to sound casual. 'Oh yes. We swapped. I gave her my….' I racked my brains trying to think of a jumper that wasn't in the ironing basket, or in the dirty washing pile. Mum always knew where everything was, and I didn't want to be caught out. '... my.... I gave her my blue and white striped one. Just for a loan. Until she comes down again. You don't mind, do you?'

Mum shook her head. 'No, darling, I don't mind. Not if it makes you feel better. Goodnight, darling.'

'Night, Mum.'

I thought she'd go then, but she didn't. She came and sat down on the bed again. 'Remember when you were very small?'

I didn't remember much about when I was very small, but sometimes it seemed like Mum remembered every tiny detail. And she loved to talk about it. At length.

She continued. 'Remember how you used to make me check under your bed every night, in case there was a monster under there?'

Oh no! Why had she suddenly brought that up? Surely she didn't suspect something? And

Mum was big on nostalgia. Was she suddenly going to try to relive old times by checking under the bed? Was this the end of everything?

I put on the most bored voice I could manage. 'That was really stupid, wasn't it?'

She smiled. 'Well, it wasn't so stupid back then. But you're a big girl now, aren't you?'

I smiled back. 'Yes, Mum. Much too big for monsters under the bed.'

She patted my shoulder. 'You're sure you don't want me to check? Just in case?'

I nodded. 'Yes, Mum. I'm quite sure.'

She sat there for a moment longer, and then to my huge relief, she stood up and walked towards the door.

I turned over, and snuggled down under the covers. Mum switched off the light and went out.

After a few seconds, Alice rolled out from under the bed. She put on a spooky voice. '*I am your worst nightmare. I am the monster from under your bed.*'

I giggled. In the dim light, I could see that she

was holding a pair of my dirty socks. 'Yuck, Meg,' she said. 'These stink. How long have they been under the bed?'

I pretended to think. 'Em.. Let me see. Oh yes, they're my communion socks. That'll be nearly four years, then.'

Alice gave a quiet little squeal. I heard the socks hitting the wall over my bed. 'Double yuck. My mum would ground me if I left my dirty washing under my bed. Still though, your mum's nice. She sounded like she really felt sorry for you.'

I sighed. 'Yeah, I know. As mums go, I suppose she's not the worst. She can be a lot of fun. And sometimes she lets us do really crazy things. Do you remember the time she let us make popcorn without putting a lid on the saucepan?'

Alice laughed. 'Oh yeah. Wasn't that mad?'

I got a sudden fit of the giggles. 'Remember how the popcorn flew everywhere, and we raced around, grabbing it, and screaming all the time?'

Alice suddenly stopped laughing. 'Yeah. Fat chance of my mum doing that. If one scrap of food touches the floor she panics, as if it was a major health alert. Your mum's great. You're lucky.'

'Mmmm ... ' I said.

Alice laughed. 'Remember the time, during the World Cup, when your mum used food colouring, and served up green, white and orange mashed potatoes for your dinner?'

I gave a wry smile. 'Hello? Did you just mention my mum, and food colouring in the same sentence? I think not.'

'But I remember it really well. She had the potatoes arranged on the plate in a perfect rectangle, and she had a stick of liquorice or something as a flag-pole.'

This time I had to laugh. 'Oh, yes, I remember all right. But Mum would sooner die than use food colouring. She probably used spinach for the green, and carrot or tomato or something to make the potatoes orange. And if I remember correctly, the flag-pole was made out of a stick of celery. It was all probably a trick to get me to eat even more vegetables.'

Alice didn't care about the details. 'Whatever. All I know is she went to loads of trouble to make dinner fun for you and Rosie.'

Suddenly I started to feel guilty for having a nicer mum than Alice. I tried to think of something not so nice about my mum. It didn't take long. I knew I was being disloyal to my mum, but it was all in a good cause.

'Hey, she's not exactly perfect, my mum. She dresses like she's trapped in the seventies. Sometimes I'm sure she thinks she's the mum in the *Alfie and Annie Rose* books.'

Alice gave a small giggle. 'Hey, now that you mention it…'

I laughed too. 'She has exactly the same hairstyle, and she's been wearing the same roundy glasses ever since I can remember. She always looks like she's just going out to dig the garden. Your mum dresses so nicely. She always looks lovely.'

Alice sighed. 'Yeah, you're right. But she's lovely in an untouchable kind of way. Jamie showed her a painting he did last week, and she kind of backed away from him, making these horrible, panicky squeals in case he'd get paint on her new white jacket. And the other day when I felt really sad about Dad, she kept going on about how she broke one of her new nails. That's not how a mum should behave. She should understand how I feel. That's her job.'

Oh dear. This wasn't working out like I planned. I decided to try again.

'Still though, whenever my mum starts to try to be all buddy-buddy, I feel really, really, embarrassed, and can't wait for her to stop. At her age she should understand the difference between being a mum and being a friend, and concentrate on the things she's good at, like turning our dinner into the Ireland flag. Don't you think so?'

Alice's voice was very quiet, and kind of sad.

'Yes, you're right. But what do you do if your mum's only good at non-mum kinds of things, like bridge, and golf, and putting on make-up?'

She gave a small sob. 'I don't think my mum even likes being a mum. Sometimes I think she's sorry she had me and Jamie. I feel like we're kind of in the way. Like we're spoiling her life.'

I didn't know what to say. Alice had never spoken like that about her mum before. She looked tearful. I leaned over and rubbed her arm. It probably didn't help very much. Alice wiped her eyes, and suddenly she spoke brightly.

'Still. We have to make our plan work. I have to get Mum back to Limerick, and then we'll all live happily ever after. Or something like that.'

I spoke fiercely. 'Our plan will work. It has to.'

Alice nodded and smiled back at me.

After that we talked about Melissa again. We talked about how vain she was, and the irritating way she was always flicking her hair, and generally swanning around the school as if she owned the place. As usual, saying bad things about her and telling each other how much she got on our nerves made us feel much better.

Then we fell asleep.

Day one was over.

Chapter twelve

Day two.

I felt kind of strange when I woke up. A bit sad. A bit happy. A bit excited. And quite a bit afraid.

Alice and I chatted quietly for a while, and then we got dressed. After that we went through the climbing in and out of the window stuff, so Alice could go to the toilet. She laughed when she got back. 'Whew, that was fun. Maybe we could invent a new sport. We could call it "bathroom mountaineering." What do you think?'

I laughed too. 'Yeah. Sounds great. We could make videos and everything. We could be rich.'

'And we could be the first world champions. We could represent Ireland in the Olympics. We…'

Just then there was a shout from the hallway. 'Megan Sheehan, are you getting up at all today? And do you want any breakfast?'

Alice scrambled under the bed, dragging her sleeping bag after her. I called out, 'Yeah, Mum. I'm on my way.' Then I heard her going back into the kitchen. Alice rolled out from under the bed, with a big grin on her face. She loved danger, and I knew she was really having fun. I often wished I could be as daring as she was.

I knew Mum would be back if I didn't appear, so after a few minutes, I wandered into the kitchen. Rosie was sitting up at the table in her patched pyjamas, eating a huge bowl of organic porridge. Poor child. She was too young to understand just how sad her life was.

Since it wasn't a school day, I was allowed to have Weetabix – supposedly a big treat. I finished my breakfast, and then I helped Mum to tidy up for a few minutes. Soon Mum went out to the utility room with some empty milk cartons for the recycling bag. Luckily, Rosie toddled after her. As soon as they were gone, I threw two Weetabix into a bowl, grabbed a spoon, and ran to my room with them.

'It's OK, it's only me.'

Alice rolled out from under the bed, and looked at the bowl I was holding towards her. She didn't seem very impressed.

'Don't worry,' I said. 'I'll get milk too. I just couldn't do it all together.'

I wandered back into the kitchen, went to the fridge and poured myself a big mug of milk.

Mum was scrubbing the porridge stains from the hob, muttering away as she did so. 'What is your dad like? At the age of thirty nine, you'd think that maybe just once he'd be able to cook porridge without letting it boil over. So much for learning through experience.'

I laughed politely, and then said, 'I'm going to read in my room for a while.'

She looked up. 'OK. Are you bringing that milk with you?'

I tried to sound casual. 'Yeah. We were doing nutrition in school last week, and Miss O'Herlihy told us all about osteoporosis. It sounds awful. I don't want to get that, so I'm going to drink two mugs of milk every day.'

Mum smiled. 'Well, I'm glad she's teaching you something useful. You know broccoli has lots of calcium too?'

I made a face. 'Yeah Mum, but that's going a bit too far, don't you think?'

She laughed, and I escaped with the milk.

Alice finished the Weetabix in double-quick time. She wiped her mouth with the back of her hand. 'Yum. I was so hungry, that was delicious.

But I don't think I can survive for the rest of the day on apples and biscuits.'

I sighed. That was going to be a bit of a problem. I'd read loads of stories where kids hide puppies, and hamsters in their bedrooms, and struggle to sneak crumbs and rasher rinds to them. I was discovering that sneaking food to a healthy twelve-year-old with a huge appetite was a bit more difficult. Already I was running out of ideas, and besides, Alice was never going to be happy with scraps.

I tried to sound positive.

'Well, don't worry. We can go out for a while this afternoon, and then we can buy you some nice stuff to eat.'

Alice sounded surprised. 'Out? How will we manage that without being caught?'

I smiled and spoke airily. 'Oh, don't worry. I have a plan.'

I felt very pleased with myself. I was getting good at all this secret stuff. Maybe I'd give up on my plans to become a vet and train to be a private investigator instead.

* * *

Al and I spent the next few hours in my room. I told Mum I was doing a big clear-out, so she wouldn't be too suspicious. I even tidied a few bookshelves, just in case she came in to check. Then Al and I sat on the floor and chatted and laughed as quietly as we could. After a while we ate some of her biscuit stash. Then, at about twelve o'clock, there was a small rattle, and when I looked around, I could see the handle of my bedroom door turning slowly. Alice was standing by the window, and had no chance to hide. I held my breath as the door opened very slowly, and . . . . . . Rosie toddled in. She beamed and held out her arms. 'Alith,' she lisped, as Alice and I stood still in panic. How could one small three-year-old spoil our great plan? It just wasn't fair.

Then I had a brainwave. I shut the bedroom door, grabbed Rosie and pulled her towards my wardrobe. 'Look, Rosie, sweeties. Lots of nice sweeties for Rosie,' I said, as I rummaged frantically for the secret bag of marshmallows I'd hidden there the week before.

Rosie loves marshmallows, so she was completely distracted for the few seconds it took Alice to roll under the bed. When Rosie's mouth was full, she turned around again. Her mouth opened in surprise, and two marshmallows popped out onto the floor.

'Alith? Alith gone?' she lisped.

I bent down and put my face near to hers, like I'd seen Mum do when she had something important to say.

'Rosie, No Alice. No Alice here. Just me and you. OK?'

She looked a bit puzzled, but happily accepted another marshmallow, and toddled off to look for Mum. I closed the door behind her, and collapsed on to the bed. Then Alice rolled out from underneath and grinned up at me.

At lunch-time, I had another moment of panic when out of the blue Rosie said, nice and clearly: 'Alith gone.'

Mum looked at her, surprised. 'Aaah. Even Rosie misses Alice. Isn't that so sweet? Yes dear, Alice has gone. But I'm sure we'll see her in a few weeks, won't we?'

I was really, really glad that Rosie was only three, and far too young to say something awful like, 'But she was in Megan's room this morning.'

As we tidied up the lunch things, I hid a few slices of bread in the pocket of my hoodie. Not very exciting food, I had to admit, but it was the best I could do under the circumstances. I could hardly bring Alice bowls of soup, or dishes of pasta, could I?

Just as I was leaving the kitchen, Mum turned to me and said, 'I've an idea, Megan. Why don't I leave Rosie with Kathleen up the road for a while, and you and I can have a nice girlie after-noon? Maybe we could go to town. We could go for hot chocolates, and than shop for some new school shoes for you. Wouldn't that be nice?'

Normally, I'd have loved that. But I could hardly skip off to town leaving Alice on her own in my room, could I? It was time for one of my special, reserve ideas. I'd joined the local tennis club a few months earlier, and whenever Mum and Dad couldn't think of anything else to complain about, they'd go on about what a waste of money it had been, since I hardly ever played. It wasn't my fault though. All the other girls who hung out there had been having private coaching since they were about six months old. They were probably playing tennis while they were still in nappies. Once, before I knew any better, Mum persuaded me to enter a competition. I can remember her encouraging smile. 'It'll be an experience, Megan, if nothing else.'

She was right. It *was* an experience. It was the most embarrassing, humiliating experience of my entire life. My opponent, Ciara, had travelled all the way from Cork for the game. Her mother and father had come with her to encourage her. (My parents hadn't thought to travel the half a mile from our house to support me. Which was just as well - I didn't need two more witnesses to my total humiliation.) Ciara had two tennis racquets, like someone who was planning to play in Wimbledon. She was dressed in designer gear from her cute white headband, down to her mega-expensive runners. And she never called when a ball went out – she just did this cool flicking thing with her fingers. After a while, when she realised just how bad I was, she started to apologise every time she sent the ball whizzing past my ear. As if apologising made it better. I only scored two points in the entire match, and that was when she double-faulted. The first time that happened, she threw her racquet on the ground in temper. If my parents saw me do that, they'd have dragged me off the court and grounded me for about six months. Ciara's mother just cooed softly to her: 'Now Ciara, don't forget about your anger management. Breathe deeply and let the tension flow away.' Sad thing was, Ciara didn't even look embarrassed.

I was put into the competition for first-time losers, but I pretended to be sick, and went home. Mum and Dad met me in the hallway. 'Well, are you our little champion?' asked Dad.

'Do we need to book tickets for Wimbledon?' asked Mum.

I shook my head, and smiled as brightly as I could. 'Oh, it was a good match, but she just about got the better of me in the end.'

I think they knew I was lying, because they didn't ask me any more.

Anyway, after that, who could blame me for being less than enthusiastic about tennis?

Still, Mum was pleased, that afternoon, when I said, 'Thanks, Mum. I'd love to spend the afternoon with you, but I was thinking of going over to the tennis club for a while. Some of the girls in my class said they might be there.'

I felt a bit mean when I saw how happy that statement made her. She gave me a big smile.

'That's great, Megan. I'm glad you're getting on with the other girls in your class. Would you like me to drop you over to the club?'

I smiled back. 'No, Mum. It's fine thanks. The walk will warm me up for the game.'

I ran to my room to change into my tracksuit and runners, and to tell Alice to get ready. A few minutes later, she climbed out the window, and I locked it behind her. Then I got my racquet from the hall cupboard, and called out, 'Bye, Mum. I'll be back in time for tea.'

She came to the door to see me off. 'Bye, darling. Have a good time.'

Luckily I'd told Alice to go out through the gate at the bottom of our back garden. I skipped down the road, and met her at the pre-arranged spot, at the end of the lane.

She stretched her arms high in the air. 'Mmmmm. It's so nice to be out. I'm beginning to feel like a prisoner. Do you think I'll be able to get a loan of a racquet at the club?'

I laughed.

'We are so not going to the tennis club!'

'Why?'

'Too many Melissas there.' (Melissa was our code word for any girl we didn't like.)

Alice looked mystified. 'Where then? Where are we going?'

I smiled.

'Into town.'

Alice was delighted. 'Hey. That's a great idea.'

I was pleased with her reaction. So pleased that I nearly forgot how much trouble I'd be in if Mum discovered I was in town without her knowing. She always said town was full of 'undesirables.' Still, sneaking Alice around was serious enough. If I was caught I was going to be in trouble anyway, and grounded for about a hundred years. I might as well have some fun and make it worth my while.

We ran to the bus stop, and arrived just as a bus pulled up. I felt very grown up indeed, as I bought two tickets, and we set off on our journey.

Chapter thirteen

We had a great afternoon in town. Somehow, everything seems much more fun when you know you're breaking every rule your parents could ever think of. (Plus lots more they haven't got around to thinking of yet.)

First stop was to get Alice a burger and chips. I wasn't hungry of course, since I'd just had lunch, but Alice acted as if she hadn't seen food for days. She stuffed her face, and then very rudely spoke through a mouthful of chips.

'Mmmm. This is so totally yum. I'd forgotten how good warm food could taste.'

I laughed. 'Well, don't get too used to it, we mightn't be able to get out again in a hurry.'

I had the biggest cup of Coke available. (Mum and Dad never allowed me to have Coke, so it tasted extra-nice.)

When Al had finished eating, and I had drained my giant Coke, we wandered out onto the street. I had an idea.

'Let's go into the supermarket. Maybe we can find something for you to eat later.' (I was feeling a bit guilty, because I knew we were having shepherd's pie for dinner, and I couldn't think of a way to smuggle some of that in to Alice.)

In the supermarket, we quickly found the shelf where all the instant-type foods were. I'd never been there before. My mum has a big thing about wholefoods, and fresh fruit and vegetables and organic stuff. Once I heard her saying to Dad that feeding ready-meals to children should be recognised as a form of child cruelty. I picked up a pot of instant noodles, and put on my mum's voice. 'Eugh! Look at this. Full of e-numbers, and hydrogenated fats. Is this food? Or is it a chemistry experiment? How *are* they allowed to get away with this?'

Alice took the pot from me and shook it. She too imitated my mum's voice. (So well that I felt a bit guilty.) 'I think it's just died. And look at this carton. How long will it take for this to decompose?'

I was glum for a moment. 'About as long as it will take my parents to forgive me, if they find out I'm in town this afternoon.'

Alice shook my arm gently. 'Don't worry, Meg, they'll never know. And anyway, we've discussed this. When my parents find me on Friday, I'm taking all the blame. I'll say everything was my fault. It was all my idea.'

I wasn't sure. 'Yes, I know you said that, but I still don't think it's fair.'

Alice spoke firmly. 'Of course it's fair. Remember, I'm the child from the broken home, not you. They'll have to make allowances for my bad behaviour. I'm just acting out my trauma.'

We selected six pots of noodly things that could be heated by pouring boiling water over them, and I tried not to worry too much about how exactly I was going to get boiling water from the kitchen into my bedroom.

After that we did a tour of Cruise's Street. In every shop that sold nail varnish, we each painted one fingernail. It took us about half an hour to get all of them done. We were slowed down quite a bit by the fact that security guards chased us out of three shops. You'd think we were 'undesirables.'

Of course, even I knew there was nothing terribly cheeky or bad about trying on nail varnish in shops, but without Alice, I wouldn't have dared. That was the great thing about Alice. When I was with her, I became a better person. I was braver. And funnier. And happier. Life was so much more fun when she was around.

We looked at CDs for a while, then jewellery and clothes. The afternoon went much too quickly. We got the bus home at half four, because I knew it would soon be dark. I also knew that if I wasn't home by dark, Mum would go to the tennis club to look for me. And if I wasn't there, she would go into totally, absolutely, crazy panic-mode. She wouldn't stop to think anything sensible, she'd just presume that I'd been kidnapped or murdered or something.

Once, in a shop, Rosie slipped out of sight for a moment and Mum nearly lost her reason. She screeched on the top of her voice. 'Rosie! Rosie! Oh my baby, what's happened to you?' Two shop assistants came running, thinking someone was dead. Then Rosie appeared from behind a rack of dresses. Mum picked her up and smothered her with big, wet, slobbery kisses. 'Oh, baby, baby. Where were you?' I thought I'd die of embarrassment, and even Rosie who should have been too young for that looked a little bit uneasy. Then, as if it wasn't quite bad enough, Melissa, with her uncanny knack for being around during my most embarrassing moments, appeared with one of her meanest buddies. They both laughed out loud, and then Melissa whispered to her friend. The only words I could hear were '*...mad mother...*' I felt like shouting at her. '*I know she's mad. But it's not my fault. Why blame me? Do you think I picked her out of a catalogue?*' But of course I didn't. I just put my head in the air and pretended not to care. (Even though of course I did. Very much.)

* * *

When we got home, Alice took the bag with the things we'd bought, and sneaked around the back of the house to wait for me to open my bedroom window. I let myself in the back door, and ruffled my hair a bit to make it look like I'd been running around the tennis court. Mum was in the kitchen as usual. She seemed to live there – like some kind of enchanted princess, condemned to a life of endless drudgery. She was straining some potatoes.

'Oh, Megan, you're back. It will be dark soon, and I was just starting to wonder about you. Did you have a nice time?'

I nodded. 'Yes, it was fine. I might go again tomorrow.'

Mum looked up this time, and smiled at me. 'Well, that is good news. Now will you please mash these potatoes for me?'

I thought of poor Alice standing in the garden in the cold, waiting for me to let her in my bedroom window. 'OK, Mum, but I'll just run out and put my racquet in the hall cupboard.'

Mum took the racquet from me before I could protest. 'It's OK, I must go check on Rosie anyway. I'll put your racquet away for you. And when you're finished the potatoes, will you empty the dishwasher, and set the table please? Dad will be home soon.'

I didn't want to arouse her suspicions by arguing. It must have been twenty minutes before I got to my room. I opened the window, and gave the signal whistle. There was no reply. I whistled again. All I could hear in reply was the rustling of the trees at the end of the garden. Then I whispered as loudly as I dared. 'Al, Al. Where are you?'

Still nothing. This was awful. Where could she have gone to?

I climbed out of the window, and ran to the bushes where Alice was supposed to wait for my whistle. She wasn't there. I suddenly began to feel a sense of panic. Where could she be? I ran around the garden, whispering her name as loudly as I dared. At last I found her sitting in Rosie's little old playhouse, right at the end of the garden. She was in a bit of a sulk, but I was so glad to see her, I didn't mind.

She spoke crossly. 'Where were you all this time? I'm frozen.'

'Sorry. Mum gave me loads of jobs. I couldn't get out of the kitchen.'

'You could have said you needed to go to the toilet, couldn't you?'

Suddenly I felt very stupid. Why hadn't I thought of that? Had I no imagination? 'Sorry, Al. I'll say that the next time.'

She brightened suddenly. 'It's OK. Now let's go in, while I can still move my fingers and toes.'

Luckily, I was first to climb in the bedroom window. I was sitting on the window-sill ready to jump down, when I realised that Mum was on her hands and knees, looking under my bed. I had just time to be grateful that we'd hidden Alice's sleeping bag and clothes in the back of my wardrobe, when Mum looked up in surprise.

'Megan! What on earth are you doing there? Were you out in the garden?'

I nodded. 'Er, yes.'

'But it's dark outside. What took you out there at this time of the evening? And why on earth are you climbing in through the window?'

I thought as quickly as my panicked brain would allow. Alice was much better at instant lies than me, but I could hardly shout out to her for ideas, could I? She was only a metre away, but I was very much on my own. I did my best.

'Em …I …you see…I ….. well, actually I….what happened was…..' Even in my panic I knew I was being totally pathetic.

For once in her life Mum didn't want a big long discussion. She stood up. 'Well, whatever. I must finish off the dinner before Dad gets here. Just get down and shut the window, and don't be so silly again.'

I jumped down and closed the window, smiling out into the darkness, just in case Alice was watching. Suddenly I was a bit worried. What had Mum been doing? Did she suddenly suspect something strange? She didn't normally look under my bed. I had to ask. 'Er, Mum, why were you looking under my bed?'

She sighed. 'I think Rosie's hidden the television remote control again. Every time I ask for it, she just laughs. She's being a right little monkey. And your dad will go crazy if it's not there when he wants to watch TV tonight.'

I gave a small sigh of relief. 'Oh, is that all? I'll help you look for it later, will I?'

Mum smiled. 'Thanks, love.'

Then she went out and closed the door, and when I was sure she wasn't coming back, I opened the window once more and let Alice in. She sat down on my bed and she didn't look terribly happy.

It was turning into a very long day.

Chapter fourteen

Dinner that evening seemed to take forever. Mum told Dad about me spending the day in the tennis club, and the two of them went on and on about it, like I'd just been awarded the Nobel Prize or something. They kept saying totally stupid things like:

'Isn't it lovely to see Megan getting some independence?'

And:

'Physical activity is so important. And tennis is *such* a lovely game.'

And:

'It's such a sociable sport. If you play tennis you'll never be without a friend.'

I was sure that if I didn't get back to my bedroom quick, I'd be without Alice as a friend, she'd be so cross and fed-up. In the end, Rosie rescued me by throwing up all over the dinner table. It was totally gross, but at least it distracted Mum and Dad for a while, so I could concentrate on thinking of a way to get boiling water in to my bedroom for Alice's noodles.

Much, much later, when I got back to my room, I still hadn't any good ideas.

'It's not my fault, Al!' I protested. 'Mum never seems to leave the kitchen. She always says she's chained to the kitchen sink, and I'm beginning to think she might be right.'

Alice wasn't sympathetic. 'Well, we'd better think of something. I'm starving.'

She picked up a pot of noodles and shook them. They made a nice rattly kind of sound. I wondered if Miss O'Herlihy would let me play them in the school band.

Alice sighed. 'This is torture. I could die of hunger here, in this very room.'

Things were getting desperate. I'd been best friends with Alice for nearly eight years, and I knew all there was to know about her. And one of the things I knew very well was that when Alice was tired or hungry, she wasn't much fun to be with.

'I know,' I said brightly. 'Mum has the hot water on for Rosie's bath. Maybe if I fill your pot from the hot tap in the bathroom, it would work.'

Alice looked a bit doubtful.

'I'm not so sure. But we'd better try something. I haven't got long left.' As she spoke she sucked her cheeks and her tummy in, and flopped onto the bed in a mock faint.

'Very funny. You just lie there being totally dramatic, and I'll do all the work,' I muttered as I stuffed a pot of noodles into the pocket of my hoodie, and went into the bathroom. I ran the hot tap for ages, but it never got that hot. Not considering I needed water that was actually boiling. In the end I got fed up, and I ripped the foil from the top of the carton anyway. Inside was really gross looking. Maybe Mum was right, it couldn't have been good for you. It didn't even look like food. It was a strange orangey colour, and was mostly dust with a layer of strange-looking brown things on top. I carefully filled the carton up to the mark on the side, and stirred it with the handle of my toothbrush. It actually smelt quite nice – a bit like pizza. I checked to see that the coast was clear, then I ran back to my room. Alice was lying on the bed, trying to look weak.

'Oh, at last. You might have to feed me. I have no strength left.'

'Here,' I said. 'Feed yourself. I worked hard for this.'

Alice took out the spoon we'd saved since breakfast, and dipped it into the pot. She stirred around, and sniffed for a while. 'Mmmm. Smells nice enough. A bit like pizza.'

I smiled to myself. 'Try some then. Before it gets cold.' What I really meant, of course, was 'before it gets colder,' since it was only barely warm to start with.

She gingerly scooped up some of the orange-brown stuff, and put it into her mouth. I smiled at her encouragingly. Behind my back I had all my fingers crossed.

'Yeeurgh.' She very rudely spat it back into its pot. 'Yuck! The noodles are still rock hard. I can't eat this. It's like eating gravel.'

I was upset. 'Come on, Al. Please try. You have to eat. It can't be all that bad.'

She thrust the pot towards my face. 'OK, You try it then.'

I shook my head. 'Sorry, I'm quite full.'

'Yeah. Full after your dinner. Was it nice? Did you have second helpings?'

All of a sudden Alice began to cry. She put her head in her hands, but I could see tears squeezing between her fingertips.

I picked up the pot and put it on my dressing table. I really didn't need to have that stuff spilled on my duvet. It looked like the kind of stuff that would make a stain that would never come out – even with the kind of biological washing powders my Mum refuses to use. 'Oh, Al. I'm sorry. Don't worry. I'll get you some food. I'll think of something, I promise. You won't starve.'

She looked at me crossly, wiping away her tears. 'I know I won't starve. But I'm not just crying about the food. It's everything. I don't think this plan is going to work. We're just going to be in terrible trouble, and then I'll have to go back to Dublin, and it will be worse than ever. Mum won't even let me visit here any more after this. Oh, Meg, this was all a huge mistake.' She put her head down again and gave a succession of huge, sad sobs.

There was no way I was giving up though. No

way. There was too much at stake.

I took her by the shoulders. 'Come on, Al. Don't talk like that. Just wait till Mum brings Rosie upstairs for bed, and I'll get some boiling water. You can have two pots of noodles, or three if you want, and you'll feel better, and then we'll plan for tomorrow. We're going to make this work. You just wait and see.'

She looked at me closely. 'Promise?'

I nodded, feeling a bit guilty because the truth of the matter was that I was no longer very sure of anything.

* * *

Later, when Mum took Rosie up for her bath, I persuaded Dad to go into the garage to look for some tennis balls for me, and I managed to get a huge jug of boiling water into my room. Alice ate three pots of noodles, and afterwards she was in much better form.

At about eight o'clock, it was time to phone Alice's mother. She answered at once.

'Alice, is that you? Where are you? I've been phoning the house for ages.'

Whew, I thought, that was lucky. Her dad must have gone out.

Alice spoke airily. 'Oh, I'm home now. Dad took me to the doctor's.'

Her mother sounded anxious. 'Doctor's? Are you that sick?'

'No, Mum. The doctor says I'm fine. It's just a bug. He says I'd better not travel for a few days yet.' She hesitated. 'Maybe I should wait until Friday, and travel up with Dad?'

She had no intention of doing that of course. The whole point was that her Dad would arrive in Dublin without her, and there would be a big panic, and her mother would be shocked into moving back to Limerick.

Her mum spoke. 'Hmmm. I don't know. It's Tuesday now, isn't it? I'll have to see. I need to speak to your father, put me on to him.'

'Well, actually, he had to go back into work. He

left early you see, to bring me to the doctor, so he had to go back in again. I think he's going to be home very late.'

Her mother sounded cross again. 'Typical. And of course the switchboard at work won't be on, will it?'

Alice grinned at me. 'No, Mum. Unfortunately not.'

Her mum made a cross, grunting kind of noise. 'And I don't suppose he's entered the twenty-first century and bought himself a mobile phone since I saw him last, has he?'

Alice grinned at me again. 'No, Mum. Sorry.'

'You know what, Alice? I think he deliberately stays out of reach.'

I think she was right. If I was married to a cross woman like her, I'd want to be out of reach occasionally too.

Alice spoke softly, like to a child. 'Don't worry, Mum. It's fine. Why don't I just tell Dad I'll stay here until Friday? He can drive me to Dublin after work and we'll see you then. Isn't that the best thing?'

Her mother gave a big, long sigh. 'Well, we'll see. Don't eat anything until you're better, and tell Dad to get you some Seven-Up to drink, and I'll ring you tomorrow.'

'OK, Mum. I'll phone you though. I've loads of credit on my mobile, and I might as well use it up.'

'OK, bye darling.'

'Bye Mum. Love you.'

Alice clicked off the phone, and grinned at me. I felt a lot better. With every passing day, and with every phone call, it seemed as if we were getting closer to our goal. If only things kept going like this, everything would be perfect. Soon Alice would be back living in Limerick where she belonged, and before long the dried noodles and the bathroom mountaineering would only be a distant memory.

Chapter fifteen

Later that night, when I was pretending to be all settled down in bed, Mum came in to say her goodnights. She still had her apron on, which meant she was busy, so I was confident it was going to be a short session.

As usual, I was wrong.

She sat on the bed and sniffed the air. 'What's that smell?'

I shrugged and tried to look innocent – a look I was beginning to perfect.

'What smell? I don't get a smell.'

I wondered was it Alice's feet. She hadn't dared to have a shower since she'd arrived in our house. And sometimes her feet did pong a bit – especially when she wore trainers.

Mum looked puzzled. 'There's definitely an unusual smell in here. It's like……'

'Maybe it's that nice perfume you and Dad gave me for my birthday. I put some on earlier.' This wasn't actually a lie. I held my wrist towards Mum's face so she could smell it.

'No, love. It's not that. It's…..'

'Or it could be nail varnish remover, or deodorant or something,' I offered helpfully.

Mum shook her head, and wrinkled up her forehead. 'No. It's nothing like that. I was going to say it's something like onions, or tomatoes or something. Only kind of artificial. Like packet soup.'

Of course. It wasn't Alice's feet that were the

problem. Mum was smelling the stupid pot noodles. She wasn't far off the mark with her guesses. I bet she was a bloodhound in her last life.

I couldn't think of anything to say. All I could think of were the empty noodle pots which were in a plastic bag in a drawer next to my bed.

She shook her head. 'Anyway, whatever that smell is, it's not very pleasant. Will I open the window and let some fresh air in?'

To open the window, she'd have had to go around to the other side of my bed, and even though Alice had rolled underneath, I didn't want to take any chances.

'No, Mum, it's fine thanks. I don't notice anything.'

She sat on the bed, and rubbed my forehead.

'Are you OK, Megan? You look a bit pale.'

I put on a brave smile. 'I'm fine. I'm a bit tired, that's all.'

For once, I wasn't lying. All the fussing over hiding and feeding Alice, and the regular bouts of bathroom mountaineering, were beginning to wear me out. I wasn't used to such an exciting life.

Mum didn't know about any of that, though, did she?

She smiled. 'That'll be all the tennis. You're just not used to it. If you play more often, you won't get so tired.'

'Mmmm. I suppose so. I think I'll play again tomorrow, and see how I get on.'

I turned over then, and snuggled under the duvet, trying to give her the hint to leave. Unfortunately, Mum was never very good at taking hints.

'And, Megan, I hope you're getting used to Alice not being around.'

I couldn't reply. This really wasn't a conversation I wanted to have at any time, and especially not right now with Alice lying under my bed listening to every single word.

Mum put on her softest voice. 'You just wait and see. You'll be in secondary school next year. You'll make lots of new friends. And in no time, you'll nearly have forgotten all about Alice. When you're all grown up, she'll just be a distant, happy memory from your childhood.'

I could feel the mattress moving slightly under my legs. Alice must have been pushing her feet up underneath it. She was making double sure that I wouldn't forget about her. It was a typical, reckless, but very funny Alice-moment.

I couldn't help it. I gave a sudden, huge laugh. Mum looked at me in surprise. I put my head in my hands and pretended to be crying.

Mum put her arms around me and rocked me. It would have been very soothing if I had been upset, but since I was trying to stifle my giggles, it wasn't very helpful. I made lots of gross snorting noises that I hoped sounded like sobs. Mum said, 'oh my poor darling,' and rocked me some more, while Alice's feet beat out a snappy little rhythm beneath the mattress.

Eventually I recovered my composure. I sat up straight, wiped my eyes and smiled a brave smile.

'I'm OK now, Mum. I just had a sudden sad moment. I was just thinking of what I'd say to Alice if I could see her now.'

While I said this, I slid my hand from under the covers and put it under the bed. As I did so I made it into a fist, in an effort to make Alice behave herself. Luckily it worked. The movement under my legs ceased, and I began to relax.

Mum got up to go.

'Better now? Call me if you need me. And remember, Megan, Daddy and I will always love you, no matter what.'

Great, I thought grimly. I'll keep that in mind for when you discover exactly how I've spent this week.

Mum kissed my forehead, and went out of the room. After waiting a few minutes, just to be sure, Alice rolled out from under the bed.

First I was angry with her but not for long, I could never be angry with Alice for long. Soon we were in fits of giggles and then we lay in the darkness without speaking.

It was nice, just knowing that she was there.

As I closed my eyes and dropped off to sleep I promised myself that Alice would never, ever be just a distant memory to me.

Chapter sixteen

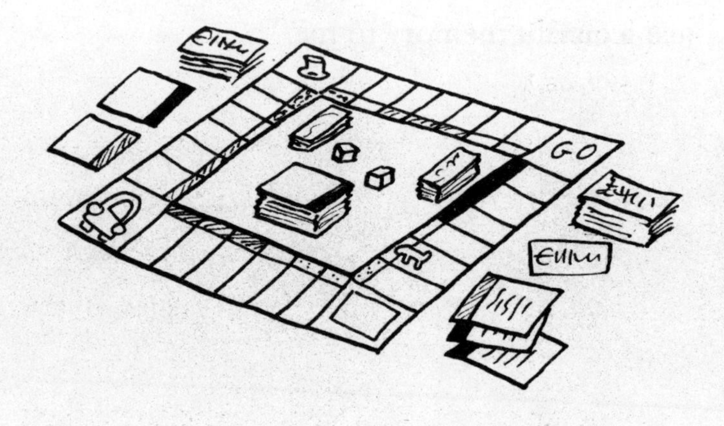

Next morning I woke up to two distinct noises. The first was the sound of heavy rain beating down on the flat roof of my bedroom. The second was the sound of Alice snoring. She sounded like a pig or a rhinoceros or something. I listened for a while, and then decided I'd better wake her. If Mum happened to pass my bedroom door, she'd surely come in, wondering what the strange noise was.

I leaned down and shook Alice hard. She woke up and looked at me in surprise, as if she wasn't quite sure where she was.

'Megan?'

I grinned at her. 'Yes, Alice. It is I.'

She looked sad. 'Sorry. I was having a very vivid dream. I thought I was at home again. With Mum and Dad. And Jamie. Jamie was being really, really stupid. But it was nice all the same.'

She sat up straight and stretched her arms high into the air. 'But no more moping. Today we are thinking positive. Today is the first day of the rest of my life.'

I laughed. 'Yes. The first day of the rest of your life in Limerick.'

'Yes! The rest of my life in Limerick.' Her face took on that shiny, happy expression that I both loved and feared.

'Bit of a problem, though,' I added.

'What's that?'

'Listen.'

She put her hand behind her ear in an exaggerated listening pose. 'What? All I can hear is Rosie crying.'

Now that she mentioned it, I became aware of a soft wailing sound coming from the other side of the house. I hadn't noticed it before. I suppose I was just so used to it. It was the background noise of my life.

'I don't mean Rosie. Can't you hear the rain?'

'So? It's raining. Big deal. This is Ireland. It rains a lot here. Hadn't you noticed? Anyway, it's not raining in here is it?'

I sighed and wondered if she was deliberately missing the point. 'Of course it's not raining in here. But how can I pretend to be going to play tennis if it's still pouring rain this afternoon? Mum knows I wouldn't play in the rain. So how will I get out of the house?'

Alice clapped one hand over her mouth in an

expression of sheer horror. I wasn't sure if she was faking it. With Alice it was often hard to tell.

She spoke in a hushed tone. 'You're right. This is a disaster. We're trapped. We could be prisoners for the whole day. It's not fair. It's cruelty to children!'

I laughed. 'Hey, it's not quite that bad. We'll think of something. Now, do you need to do some mountaineering before I go for breakfast?'

She shook her head. 'No. I'm fine. Ill wait till you get back.'

I shrugged, and pulled on my dressing gown.

'OK. I'll see you in a while. I'll bring you back something nice.'

Then, closing the door carefully behind me, I went back to my real life.

* * *

After breakfast, Mum said. 'You know what day today is, Megan?'

I pretended to think. 'Wednesday?'

Of course I knew perfectly well what day it

was. Wednesday was an important day. It was half way through the week. Alice had been in hiding for two days, and we only needed to continue for two more.

Mum continued. 'Well, Wednesday is toddler group day. Rosie and I will be leaving in a few minutes. It starts at half ten.'

At these words, Rosie began to jump up and down. I felt like doing the same. Mum going out was an unexpected bonus.

Rosie clapped her fat little hands together. 'Yay. Toddle oop. Toddle oop. Bikkies. Juice.'

Poor Rosie. She had no freedom at all, and the only time she ever saw a biscuit was at toddler group.

Mum laughed, and stroked Rosie's hair. 'Well, Rosie's excited about it anyway. Why don't you come, Megan? You can play with the toddlers. You always like that.'

I shook my head. 'I don't think so, Mum. I'm a bit old for that stuff.'

'OK, you can stay here then. But no television and no computer. You can tidy the family room while I'm gone.'

I smiled my sweetest smile. 'OK. Leave it to me. Your wish is my command.'

Mum did her usual half-exasperated shake of her head, and then she went to get her coat. I did the good girl act, and began to stack the dishwasher.

As Mum was leaving she came back into the kitchen. 'Sure you won't come?'

'Yup. Quite sure.'

'OK, so. Be good. I have to go to the supermarket on the way home, so I won't be back until about one.'

I had to bend my head over the dishwasher so she wouldn't see how happy that news made me. My hair fell down into a dirty porridge bowl, but I didn't even care.

As soon as Mum's car was gone from the drive, I skipped into my room.

'It's OK. It's me.'

Alice rolled out from under the bed.

I threw my arms in the air with a theatrical flourish.

'Ta-da! May I present you, Alice O'Rourke, with the freedom of this house? For two and a half long hours, you, Alice O'Rourke can wander the rooms of this dwelling without fear of discovery, or banishment to Dublin.'

Alice looked at me, puzzled. 'Quit the fancy stuff. Just tell me what's happening.'

'My mum's gone out,' I explained. 'We're free.'

Alice jumped up. 'Free, and starving. Take me to your kitchen.'

It was strange, sitting in the kitchen with her, watching her eat two bowls of Weetabix, and three slices of toast. She kept getting up from her seat, and wandering into the hall, as if she had never experienced such freedom before.

Then we tidied the kitchen together, and we worked as fast as we could to get the family room tidy enough to keep Mum off my back. After that, the rain stopped for a short while, and we played swingball in the back garden, where we were safe from neighbours' prying eyes.

When it started to rain again, we went back inside. I had a brainwave. I dug out an old vacuum flask from one of the kitchen cupboards, and filled it up with boiling water. Then I hid it in my room, so Alice could use it later, to heat up her noodles. I was very pleased with myself, and even Alice was impressed.

I wanted to listen to music in my room, but that wasn't really fair on Alice, who'd seen more than enough of my room over the last few days. So instead we lay on the floor in the family room, and we played Monopoly.

It was nice. Every now and then I was able to forget for a moment what was really going on, and for those few seconds, it was just like old times. Sometimes I half expected, Alice to jump up saying it was time for her to go home for lunch, promising to be back within twenty minutes. Sometimes I thought Mum might just casually look in and offer us some wonderful treat like salt-free rice cakes or organic carrot sticks. Sometimes I thought Rosie would toddle in and sit on Alice's back, one of her favourite places. So sometimes during that game of Monopoly, I was very, very happy. And sometimes I was very sad.

I was being especially careful, checking my watch every few minutes, making sure it wasn't time for Mum to come home. It was only five past twelve when I threw a three, and landed on one of Alice's streets that had a hotel on it. She jumped up and did a triumphant little jig. "Pay up, sucker. You owe me fifteen hundred euro."

I was riffling through my money to see if I had enough to pay her, when to my complete horror, I heard a very familiar sound.

It was the distinctive, unmistakable chug-chug noise of my mother's old banger of a car pulling into the driveway.

Chapter seventeen

I went into instant, total panic mode. I stood in the middle of the floor and flapped my arms like a frightened chicken who'd been drinking too much Cola. This could be the beginning of a major disaster. To get back to my room, Alice would have to run past the glass front door and Mum would surely see her.

'Quick, hide!' I hissed.

Alice looked really pale. 'Hide? Where?' Her voice was all squeaky and scared.

I looked around the room. There weren't

many choices. It was a small room, and Alice is a big, tall girl. 'Behind the couch, quick!'

She'd just hidden herself, when Mum walked in with Rosie in her arms. She sat on the couch.

'Oh, what a cross bunny this one is today. She must be teething.'

She looked at the game of Monopoly, still spread out all over the floor. There had been no time to clear it away.

'Megan, what on earth have you been doing? Why is that all over the floor?'

I sighed, hoping it would keep the panic from my voice. 'Oh, I got bored. I wanted to see if you could play Monopoly on your own. You can't, actually.'

That was a fairly weak explanation, so I tried to change the subject. 'You're home early.'

'Mmmm, I know. I couldn't face the supermarket with Rosie like this. I'll go later, after she's had her nap.'

Luckily, at the mention of the word 'nap'

Rosie cuddled into Mum's arms and sucked her thumb. Mum got up slowly so as not to disturb her. 'I'll put her up now, poor little lamb.'

Mum had only got as far as the hall when the doorbell rang. 'Get that, will you, love?' she said over her shoulder as she went upstairs.

I went and opened the door. It was horrible, nosy old Mrs O'Callaghan from up the road.

What a treat!

Not.

'Mum's upstairs,' I said, hoping she'd go away.

She gave me a stern look. 'Why don't I just come in and wait then?'

She didn't wait for an answer. She swept past me and went into the family room, plonking her huge fat behind onto the couch. I winced. Alice must have felt the force of that.

Mum came back down. 'Geraldine. How nice to see you.'

Hah! And Mum gives me grief for telling lies. I was convinced that she hated Mrs O'Callaghan as much as I hate Brussels sprouts.

Mrs O'Callaghan settled herself further into her seat. 'Well it's not a social call, Sheila. I'm here on residents' association business.'

I watched as Mum's face fell even further. Mum believed in changing the world. For her the residents' association was far too small and unimportant.

Mrs O'Callaghan wittered on for about half an hour about stupid stuff like leaves on foot-paths and whether parking should be confined to one side of the street. I sat in the corner of the room and pretended to read. I didn't feel it fair to abandon Alice even though there was nothing I could do to help her to escape.

Finally, Mrs O'Callaghan stopped talking. She stood up and went towards the door. Then she stopped and peered at Mum over her thick glasses. 'Do you ever see poor Peter from next door?'

I looked up from my book, alarmed. Peter was Alice's father.

Mum shrugged. 'No, not that much.'

Mrs O'Callaghan took a deep breath, and then launched into a tirade. 'Well, that poor, poor man. How that despicable Veronica could just up and leave him, I just don't know. Of course she was always a nasty piece of work. I saw that the first day she moved in. Limerick was never good enough for her, with her designer-this and her designer-that, and her fancy Dublin ways. She thought she was better than the rest of us, and she's nothing better than a tramp. Good riddance to her, is what I say. We're all better off without her around.'

I sat still in my chair. I couldn't move. All I could think of was poor Alice, listening to these awful comments about her mother. If this was a horror movie, Alice would leap from behind the couch, launch herself on top of Mrs O'Callaghan, and scratch her eyes out. Fortunately for Mrs O'Callaghan, this was real life, and Alice stayed hidden.

I looked towards my mum. I knew she shared Mrs O'Callaghan's opinions about Alice's mum, but could I rely on her not to say so?

I held my breath. Mrs O'Callaghan folded her arms, carefully holding up her huge floppy chest. She too was waiting for a reply.

Finally my mum spoke. 'Well, Geraldine, I try not to judge others. I always found Veronica to be perfectly nice and polite.'

I could have run over and hugged my mum, but that might have aroused her suspicions, so I resisted. Mrs O'Callaghan unfolded her arms and rearranged her chest. She didn't like to be disagreed with. 'Well then, it's time I left, I'm sure. Goodbye, Sheila. Goodbye, Megan.'

She went out, looking rather offended, and banged the front door behind her.

Mum went upstairs to check on Rosie. I ran back to the family room, and hauled Alice from behind the couch. We ran to my room and closed the door behind us.

Alice sat on the bed. She wiped her eyes when she thought I wasn't looking, but I could see that she was upset. I put one arm around her. 'Don't mind that nasty old woman. She's only jealous. She's just a big ugly hag, and what does she know about anything?'

Alice shrugged. 'You're right. And I'm glad your mum defended my mum. It's nice to know that my mum still has some friends around here.'

I nodded. Luckily Alice didn't know that Mum only defended Veronica because she knew it would make Mrs O'Callaghan so cross.

Suddenly Alice looked really serious. 'You know what, Megan?'

'What?'

'I don't care what Mrs O'Callaghan thinks. I don't care what anyone thinks. All I care about is getting away with this for two more days. All I care about is making this plan work, and shocking my mother into moving back to Limerick. That's it. That's all.'

She kicked off her shoes and lay down on the bed. 'Now what?'

I sat down beside her. 'I think we should stay in here out of trouble. I've had quite enough shocks for one day.

Alice nodded. 'Yes, you're right. Let's stay here, and we'll have a nice quiet afternoon.'

Sometimes it's scary how very wrong you can be.

Chapter eighteen

It was about two o'clock and Al and I were in my room playing cards when the front doorbell rang.

Mum called from upstairs. 'Get that, Megan please, will you? I'm in the middle of tidying Rosie's room.'

I sighed. 'OK, Mum.' I hoped it wasn't that old battleaxe Mrs O'Callaghan back with more of her nasty opinions. I'd had more than enough of her for one day.

I got up and went out into the hall. I could see two adult-sized figures through the frosted glass of the front door. Maybe Mrs O'Callaghan had brought reinforcements. Maybe she was going to use brute force to threaten us into caring about the parking situation on our road. Then I thought not. Even she wasn't that stupid.

It was probably political canvassers, I decided. Mum wouldn't be pleased. She always felt she had to argue with these guys, instead of just promising them all she'd vote for them, like Dad did.

I wondered if I could get rid of them without Mum knowing they'd ever been there. I rehearsed a speech in my head. I opened the door. And then I felt like shutting it again very quickly, because there, in living colour, on my front doorstep, stood Alice's parents. And they didn't look very happy. In fact they looked very annoyed indeed.

I looked at them and they looked at me. Then we looked at each other some more. I got a very sick feeling in my stomach. I wished I could be somewhere, anywhere else. At school. At the dentist. On the street being teased by Melissa. Anywhere would have been better than on my own doorstep, waiting for my world to crash down around me.

Al's mum, Veronica, spoke. Her voice was cold and sharp. 'Where's Alice?'

'Alice?' I repeated.

'Yes, Alice,' she snapped. 'My daughter.'

Alice's dad, Peter, gave a small cough. 'Our daughter actually.'

Veronica gave him an evil look, and repeated. 'Where is Alice, *our* daughter?'

I stood there for a moment with my mouth open. I couldn't think of anything to say. It didn't matter anyway. I was too shocked to speak. I opened my mouth and closed it again. No sound came out, not even the usual babble that pops out when I'm nervous.

Veronica continued. 'And if you're trying to think of a silly little lie - don't bother. You would only be wasting your time. We know she's here. Get her. Now.'

Her nasty tone convinced me that this wasn't a time for pretending not to understand what she meant.

'OK,' I whispered, and I went to my room. Veronica followed me.

Alice was sitting on the bed, pale-faced. Obviously she'd heard her mother's voice. Veronica's icy tones would cut easily through any walls. And when her mum spoke like that, Alice probably figured that hiding under my bed wasn't going to be much use.

She spoke weakly. 'Hi, Mum.'

Her mother didn't answer. She caught Alice rather roughly by the arm, and led her towards the front door. I followed, not quite sure what to do or say. As we arrived in the hallway, Mum appeared at the top of the stairs with an armful of dirty sheets. 'Who was at the door, Meg?' she began to say, before she spotted the four of us in the hall. She took a few steps towards us, and then she did something that really, really, annoyed me. She dropped the sheets on the stairs, and began to smooth her hair. I really, really, hated that. (Even though I'd often heard her mocking Alice's mum behind her back for all the time she spent on her appearance, Mum always seemed ill-at-ease, and almost shy in her presence. As if secretly she felt bad for not being as glamorous as her.)

And anyway, smoothing her hair was a total waste of time. Mum still looked like she'd been dragged backwards through a bush.

Then she embarrassed me further, by completely misunderstanding the scene.

'Veronica, Peter, how nice to see you. Hello,

Alice dear, have you come back for another few days? How nice. Megan has been missing you. Now, won't you all come in and have something to drink? We have some very nice herbal teas. They have no caffeine you know.'

Veronica looked at Mum as if she were a complete, raving lunatic.

'No, thank you, Sheila. This isn't a social call, you know. These two girls have been very, very deceitful.'

Mum looked at me. 'What exactly is happening here?' she asked.

I thought it wiser not to answer that question. Anyway, Veronica seemed happy to speak for me. She looked at Mum. 'I take it from your reaction that you didn't know Alice was here?'

Mum shook her head, and Veronica continued. 'Well, then it's even worse than I thought. She must have been hiding.'

Mum looked puzzled. She was normally quite smart, but on this occasion, she was very slow to understand what was going on. She spoke to Alice. 'Hiding? But….'

Veronica interrupted. 'She was supposed to be in Dublin with me, but instead she was here, hiding.'

Mum still looked confused. Then she nodded and gave a small smile as if she understood. Of course she didn't. 'Oh, I see, Alice. You were hiding next door, while your dad was at work. I suppose that was a bit bold. Your mother must have been worried sick.'

Veronica's face began to go a very strange pink colour, a bit like my strawberry shower gel. Only without the sparkly bits.

'No, Sheila. She wasn't hiding in her house. She was hiding in yours. It might be news to you that my daughter has spent the last few days hiding under your roof. Though how you couldn't have noticed, is quite beyond me'

Mum scratched her head vigorously. Great, as well as bad hair, now Veronica probably thought

Mum had headlice too.

Mum looked at me. 'Is this true, Megan?'

I nodded.

Mum scratched her head again. Veronica took a small step away from her.

Mum spoke. 'But why? You could have had Alice to stay if you liked. You only needed to ask. There was no need to hide.'

Veronica spoke coldly. 'I wouldn't have permitted it, Sheila. Her home is in Dublin now. Alice belongs with me. And I'd like to point out that I have a very busy schedule. I have lots more to do than driving down here to reclaim my errant daughter. I have to say this is all very inconvenient.'

That made me really, really cross. Alice's world was falling apart, and all her mother could think of was her schedule. She probably had to cancel a hair appointment or a session at the nail bar or something. I felt like hitting her, or stamping my foot or something, but since I was in enough trouble already, I just held my breath and looked at the ground.

Just then, Rosie appeared down the stairs. 'Alith,' she said, and she put her hands up to Alice, hoping to be picked up. Alice just rubbed her hair in a distracted kind of way. Rosie persisted, jumping up and down, repeating, 'Alith, Alith, up.' Mum picked Rosie up and cuddled her.

I put my head down. Suddenly it was clear to me that Alice and I had been wasting our time. Our plan was never going to work. There was no hope of her moving back to Limerick. Alice could have stayed hidden in my room for weeks, or even months, but still it would have made no difference. Nothing we did would ever change her mum's mind.

And then I started to cry. I knew that Alice had more reason to cry than me, but she just stood quietly between her mother and her father, saying nothing. I couldn't stop crying though. Big fat tears rolled down my face, and dripped onto my sweatshirt. I felt sad and angry and small and stupid. Mum put one hand on my shoulder, and squeezed it gently.

That small gesture gave me the courage to speak. I took a deep breath and the words came tumbling out. 'All we wanted was for Alice to come back here to Limerick. It's not fair. All her friends are here. Her dad is here. She's supposed to be at school here. This is her home. She shouldn't have to leave. It's wrong. It's cruel.'

I looked at Veronica. 'How could you do this to her? If you loved her, you wouldn't make her leave.'

I stopped then. I wasn't sorry I'd said the words, but I was very afraid at what would happen next.

Veronica took a step towards me. Her high heels clicked loudly on the wooden floor. She held up one hand. Her fingernails were painted with perfect black and white stripes. For a moment, I thought she was going to hit me. Then she stepped back again. 'You're two very silly, immature, selfish girls. You only think of yourselves.'

Just like you then, you nasty cow.

This time I kept the words inside my head.

Veronica spoke quietly. 'Come on, Alice, come with me.'

With that she pulled Alice by the arm, and they headed off down our garden path, and towards Alice's house.

'Bye-bye, Alith,' said Rosie. But Alice didn't look back.

Alice's dad, Peter, was still hovering awkwardly in the hall. Mum looked at him. 'I'm sorry about all this, Peter. I had no idea what was going on, you know.'

He smiled, a tired kind of smile. 'Of course, Sheila. It wasn't your fault, or Megan's I'm sure. Alice is very strong-willed, you know. And the move has been very upsetting for her. It's been upsetting for all of us. We….'

He stopped. Then he smiled a sad kind of

smile. 'Well, thanks. I'd better go home and see what's happening.' I had a funny feeling he'd have been happier to stay there in our hallway, where it was warm and safe.

Mum spoke again. 'Before you go, Peter, please tell me one thing. How did you know Alice was here?'

He shrugged. 'I went to the tennis club for a drink last night, and one of the lads mentioned that his daughter had seen Megan and Alice on the Ennis Road, yesterday afternoon. Of course, I said he must have been mistaken, that Alice was in Dublin with her mother. But then Veronica phoned me at work first thing this morning, with a rambling story about Alice staying with me because she was sick. Well, it didn't take us long to work things out. She was rather angry - well, you probably saw that for yourself. She left Jamie with a friend and she drove down immediately. She's going back in a few minutes, I expect.'

Mum looked at me. 'Megan, has Alice left stuff in your bedroom?'

I nodded.

'Well, go and pack up her things and give them to Peter.'

I went without speaking. It only took a few minutes to roll up Alice's sleeping bag, and put her clothes into her bag. Then I grabbed a piece of paper and wrote a quick note.

Bye, Alice. Sorry it didn't work out. Hope you're not in too much trouble. I'll miss you. Meg.

A few tears even fell onto the page, which was really sad, but I had no time to write a new note, so I shoved it under her clothes, and closed the bag.

Peter took the bag from me and left. Mum closed the door behind him. She looked at me, and said nothing. I wasn't quite sure how cross she was. She had a strange expression on her face that I couldn't read. This time, even she couldn't say, 'something just like this happened me when I was about your age.' So she said nothing. I thought about all the lies I'd told her over the past few days. I wiggled my foot on the hall mat. There was a hole in my sock. I couldn't help wondering if Mum saw it, would she want to darn it?

I said. 'Maybe I should go to my room for a while.'

Mum looked at me.

'Yes, maybe you should. We'll have a long talk about this when your father gets home.'

I went to my room, and lay on the bed. I could see the flask of hot water on the windowsill, all ready for Alice's tea. She wouldn't need it now.

After a while, I could hear voices from the front of the house. I went out into the hall and opened the front door. Alice and her mum were just about to drive away. Peter was standing on their front step, looking very serious. Then he turned around and went back into the house.

Alice wasn't crying, but she was awfully pale,

and sad looking. She looked up and saw me. She gave me a small wave, and I waved back. I could see her mum's lips moving, but Alice didn't turn towards her. She kept looking at me. We waved until they were out of sight, and then I went back into my room to wait until Dad got home.

Chapter nineteen

Much, much later I heard Dad coming in from work. I heard Mum talking to him in the hall, and then they went in to the family room. They were there for ages. Dad probably wanted to watch a match on television, but I figured Mum wouldn't have let him. I knew they were talking about me.

After the longest time, there was a knock on my bedroom door. It was Mum, Dad, and Rosie.

Great, I thought, a family conference. *Subject: How long should Megan be grounded for? All offers over thirty years will be considered.*

> *Questions for discussion:*
> *1. Should she be allowed out for her confirmation?*
> *2. Should she be allowed to watch television at any time between now and the opening ceremonies of the 2050 Olympics?*
> *3. Should she be allowed out for her graduation dance?*
> *4. Should she be allowed to have a mobile phone this side of her hundredth birthday?*

I sat on the edge of my bed, and Mum and Dad sat on either side of me. Did they think I was going to make a run for it? Where would I go? Was I going to escape to Dublin and hide under Alice's bed until I was old enough to go to college? Hardly.

Rosie sat on the floor and started to play with my jewellery box. She emptied it out onto the carpet. I didn't care. I had more to worry about than my necklaces getting tangled or my earrings getting lost.

Mum spoke first. 'Have you anything to say, Megan?'

I hated that. Surely she'd discovered that tactic in one of those parenting books she was forever reading. I always felt it put me at a disadvantage in our discussions.

I decided to be brief.

'I'm sorry, Mum. Sorry, Dad.'

Dad looked me in the eye. 'Sorry? Is that it?'

I spoke again. 'Well, what else do you want me to say? I am sorry. Sort of. Can't you see? I only did it because I miss Alice so much. And she misses me. It's not fair. She should be here. Not in some stupid old apartment in Dublin. She belongs here, and all we want is for her to come back. Is that so bad?'

Mum spoke softly. 'Of course that's not bad. But you can't get involved. You can't change people's lives. It was a very silly thing to do. Her parents might have panicked. The guards could have been involved. It might have been a lot more serious than it was.'

Dad joined in. 'Her parents have to live their lives, and even though it makes you sad, there's not a lot you can do. It's tough, but sometimes kids just have to grin and bear it. That's just the way life is. You'll understand better when you're older.'

Mum and Dad had a lot to say. An awful lot. And it took them an awful long time to say it. There was a lot of talk about responsibility, and maturity and that kind of stuff. They weren't really cross, though. And they never raised their voices.

But after twenty minutes of meaningful discussion, I was bored out of my mind. In fact I was beginning to think that I'd prefer to be shouted at for five minutes, and given a proper punishment, and get it over with.

In the end, Mum and Dad decided that as a punishment I'd have to empty the dishwasher every day for a week, and vacuum the whole house every three days for a month. I looked at them in surprise. That wasn't much of a punishment. I did those jobs most of the time anyway. And more besides.

Mum and Dad stood up. Dad patted me on the shoulder, and said, 'Don't worry, Meggie.'

Mum gave me an intense kind of look. 'Sometimes you have to be seen to do something,' she said. Then they went out.

I puzzled over her words for a while, before a light went on in my brain and I knew what she meant. Mum and Dad needed to be able to say that I'd been punished, just in case they met any of Alice's family, and were asked how they'd dealt with the situation.

I smiled to myself. Maybe they weren't the worst parents in the world after all. OK, so in an ideal world, I'd have preferred ones who were a bit more generous with the chocolate and the electronic toys, and a bit less keen on vegetables and household chores, but I suppose you can't have everything.

After that we had dinner together. It was chicken with pasta, my favourite. As I ate, I found I was a little relieved that I wouldn't have to sneak back into my room afterwards to organise Alice's noodles. I was glad I wouldn't have to spend twenty minutes climbing in and out of the bathroom window. I was looking forward to just chilling out on the couch and watching TV with Mum and Dad and Rosie.

And then I felt really, really guilty.

Before bed, I asked Mum if I could check my e-mails. She nodded. 'OK, love, but don't be too disappointed if there's none from Alice. Her Mum is really very cross with her. She might not be in a position to be e-mailing anyone.'

Mum was wrong though. There was a message. A big, long one.

Hi Megan,

I've got good news and bad news. The bad news is, I'm not allowed to e-mail you for four weeks. The good news is, Mum plays bridge three nights a week, and won't ever know if I obey her or not. And Jamie's asleep, so he'll never know either so I won't even have to bribe him to keep quiet. I hope you didn't get into too much trouble. I know I said I'd take all the blame, but when Mum and Dad showed up, I got such a fright, I forgot all about it. When we went into our house, Mum really lost it. She was shouting and screaming at me for ages. Then the usual thing happened. She started to blame Dad, and she was shouting at him as if I wasn't there. I wanted to tell him to defend himself, and not to let her talk to him like that, but I was too scared. Then, after ages, Mum started one of her 'poor me' acts. She said, 'After all I've done for this family, how could you do this to me?' And then something fantastic happened - Dad went really crazy. He doesn't usually get cross, but this time he really lost it. It was scary but great. He said all Mum had ever done for the family was ruin it, and that Jamie and me are going to end up as delinquents, and it will all be her fault. Dad really got going then. He called her a big, selfish social climber. He said he was going to put his foot down once and for all. In the end it was really, really great. I was so proud of him. He said if Mum didn't promise to let me and Jamie go to Limerick every second weekend, and for half of all holidays, he'd hound her through the courts and have her declared an unfit mother. Mum was quiet for once. I think she got a bit of a fright. And you know, she's not as bad as Dad says. She just needs more space in her life. I think I can kind of understand that. Then Dad made her promise that we can come down the weekend after next, and guess what? She promised. And I'll be down for a full week at Christmas, and lots of times in between. So you see, Megan, we won. It worked!!!!!! Thanks to you, I can spend lots of time at home, and even though it's not as good as moving back home for good, I think even I have to admit that it was very unlikely that that was ever going to happen. I was just dreaming as usual.

Thanks for your note. It made me feel both better and worse. But who cares? Let's look on the bright side of things. I'll see you in just nine more days, which is less than a week and a half away. And I won't even have to sleep on the floor, or eat dried noodles or climb out a single window.

Yippee!!!!!

Al

It was late, so I just sent her a short reply.

Al

That is the best news in the whole wide world.

Meg

PS: You will never be a distant memory.

I wasn't sure about the last line. Maybe it was a bit OTT. But then I decided to leave it in. Alice and I had been through a lot in the past few days. I knew she'd understand.

I shut down the computer, and went to bed. Mum came in to kiss me. She even joked about Alice. 'Do I need to check under the bed tonight? Anyone else in the room, besides you?' she asked.

I shook my head. 'Just me, I promise.'

Mum hugged me, and then put out the light.

It had been a very long day.

Chapter twenty

It's the day after Christmas Day.

Soon Alice will be arriving to stay with her dad for ten long, lovely days. Her mum is going to Lanzarote, for a break. My mum laughed when she heard that, and said that it must be nice to need a break from bridge and tennis and going to the beautician's, but then she realised that I was listening so she didn't say any more. It wasn't a mean laugh though, and I didn't mind.

I'd better go back and give a quick account of what happened next.

Going back to school after mid-term was nearly as bad as September had been. But then, over the next few weeks, things started to improve. One day I noticed that Grace and Louise, two of Melissa's friends, didn't seem to be talking to her. I wondered why, but of course I didn't ask them. That night I e-mailed Alice to tell her. She replied that it was probably because they didn't curtsey low enough when they were talking to her. Then I e-mailed back and said that they probably forgot to admire her hair, or her new coat or something. Anyway, I didn't care what they were fighting about, it was nice to know that that there existed two more people who understood that Melissa wasn't the most wonderful creature on this earth.

Next day, Miss O'Herlihy decided to move our places in class again. She put Melissa next to

Jane, and everyone laughed. Melissa looked really, really mad, but couldn't say anything because Miss O'Herlihy had her very cross face on. Jane just sat up straight, and said nothing. I felt kind of sorry for her. (Not sorry enough to want to sit with her again though.)

Then Miss O'Herlihy put me next to Louise. I would have hated that before, but it turned out that Louise was really quite nice. At break-time she shared her crisps with me. And when I told her a joke, she laughed like she really thought it was funny.

A few days later, we were told to divide into three for history projects. Louise suggested that Grace, me and her would go together. I was delighted, but tried to look cool, like it was no big deal. We decided to do our project on the Vikings. We worked on it for two weeks. Grace and Louise came to my house most days after school, and we looked stuff up on the Internet. Mum made us celery and carrot sticks, and

Grace and Louise were really nice and didn't laugh once.

When the project was finished we all went to Grace's house for a pizza, to celebrate. It was fun.

At first, I didn't know what to say to Alice about my new friends. I didn't want her to be jealous. I didn't want her to think that I had already forgotten about her.

I needn't have worried though. She thought it was great that I wasn't on my own any more. She said that made her feel better about making new friends in Dublin.

One weekend when she was staying with her dad, Alice asked Grace, Louise and me over for an evening. We watched a video, and played basketball, and just did girlie kind of stuff. It was great.

That Sunday, when she was leaving to go back to Dublin, I felt extra bad. I told her so.

She gave a big laugh. 'Don't worry. I'll be fine. I'm invited to a sleepover in Dublin on Friday, and on Saturday a few of us are going to the pictures in the afternoon. I'll miss you. But I'll get over it.'

I laughed too.

She gave me a quick hug. 'And I'll see you the week after next.'

As her dad drove her away, I forgot even to feel sad.

* * *

So there it is.

I hope that even when I'm a grown-up, Alice will be my very best friend. Grace and Louise are nice, but they'll never replace Alice. We've decided that we both want to go to college together, and we're going to share a flat. Alice says she'll live with me forever as long as I promise not to feed her with dried noodles. I agreed, but made her promise to do something about her snoring.

Alice says she probably won't get married, after seeing how her parents turned out, but if ever she changes her mind, then she'd like me to be her bridesmaid.

I hope Alice and I will be very best friends when we're ninety, and shuffling round a nursing home in baggy brown cardigans and furry slippers, talking about hearing aids and walking sticks and stuff.

But in the meantime, I'm having fun.

Read an extract from the second book about best friends Megan and Alice!

Alice Again

by Judi Curtin

It's spring mid-term, and Alice has invited Megan to visit her in Dublin. Megan is hoping for a nice trouble-free few days with her best friend. But no such luck! She discovers that Alice is once again plotting and scheming.

Alice tells Megan that her mum Veronica has a new boyfriend. She wants to find out who the mystery man is and get rid of him. She involves Megan in her plan, and Megan soon finds herself caught up in a series of strange events ...

Chapter three

Soon we were at Alice's apartment. Jamie immediately parked himself in front of the television, and Veronica went into the kitchen. Alice brought me into her bedroom, and closed the door behind us.

I sat on her bed and picked up a furry purple cushion. Alice always has loads of cushions on her bed. (My mum says cushions are just holiday camps for dust mites, and doesn't let me have any.) I played with the cushion's silky fringe while I waited for Alice to talk. I was dying to know what was going on, but with Alice, it's always better to pretend not to be too eager.

After a moment she spoke. 'Mum has a boyfriend.'

I opened my mouth, but no words came out. What on earth could I say to that? A mum having a boyfriend just sounded too weird. Big sisters and babysitters and pop stars had boyfriends. Not mums. I couldn't picture my mum with a boyfriend. I couldn't imagine her with anyone except for Dad. It just wouldn't seem right. But then, maybe that's what Alice used to think about her parents before they separated. For a moment I was glad that my mum was all scruffy and worn-down looking. Surely she could never get a boyfriend even if she wanted one?

Alice stood in front of me with her arms folded. She sounded cross. 'Didn't you hear me, Megan? My mum has a boyfriend.'

I still didn't know what to say. I didn't have a whole lot of experience of this kind of thing. 'Oh ... em ... that's.... well ... I mean ... I'm sorry. I'm sorry to hear it,' I muttered.

Was that the right thing to say? Probably not. It didn't seem like enough, and Alice certainly didn't look very pleased. I racked my brains for some sensible questions. After a few seconds, they all poured out in a rush.

'How do you know? Did she tell you? Who is he? Have you met him? What's he like? Is he nice?'

Alice shook her head, but I had no idea which of my many questions she was saying 'no' to. She looked all worked up and sad. I patted the bed beside me, the way Mum sometimes does with Rosie. Alice obediently sat down beside me. I spoke softly. 'Just tell me everything.' At least if she talked, I didn't have to.

Alice took a deep breath. 'OK. Well, like I said, Mum has a boyfriend. She hasn't actually told me yet, but I know she has.'

For a moment I felt a bit better. Alice's vivid imagination was legendary. Maybe it wasn't true at all. I spoke again. 'So how exactly do you know?'

She gave a sad laugh. 'Any fool could see it. He rings her every night. Always at seven o'clock. Just when *The Simpsons* is starting. It's been going on for ages. The first time I answered it, and it was a man's voice. Now Mum grabs the phone before Jamie and I can get there. Then she goes all shy and breathy, and she keeps fixing her hair, and she takes the phone into her room so we won't hear what she's saying.' ...

She stopped talking, and I thought she was going to cry. At that moment I really hated Veronica. She'd messed up Alice and Jamie's lives. And even my life had changed forever when she decided to drag half her family off to live in Dublin. What on earth could I say that would make this better? ...

Then, all of a sudden Alice's mood changed. She gave me a huge smile. It was a smile that I knew very well indeed. It was a smile that made me very, very nervous. I held my breath and waited.

She jumped up from the bed. 'Anyway, I'm so glad you're here, Meg. Everything's going to be fine now that you're here. The timing's perfect.'

'What exactly do you mean?'

She smiled at me again. 'You can help me.'

I could hardly get the words out, 'Help you what?'

She spoke as calmly as if she was asking me to help tidy her room, or help her with her maths homework.

'You can help me to find out who Mum's boyfriend is.'

I allowed myself a small sigh of relief. That wasn't really so bad. In fact, it was almost harmless. It might even be fun.

Then Alice continued, 'And once we know who he is, we can get rid of him.'

* * *